BEST
GAY
ROMANCE
2012

BEST
GAY
ROMANCE
2012

EDITED BY
RICHARD LABONTÉ

Published in the United States by Cleis Press Inc., 2246 Sixth Street, Berkeley, California 94710.

Printed in the United States.
Cover design: Scott Idleman/Blink
Cover photograph: Ed Freeman/Getty Images
Text design: Frank Wiedemann
First Edition.
10 9 8 7 6 5 4 3 2 1

Trade paper ISBN: 978-1-57344-758-4
E-book ISBN: 978-1-57344-768-3

For Asa. Who else?
Love you.

CONTENTS

INTRODUCTION:
THE HEART FINDS MANY WAYS

After reading several hundred submissions for the *Best Gay Romance* series—this is the fifth I've edited—I've compiled a mental checklist of recurring romantic themes, including (but certainly not limited to):

Young love. Love, unexpected. Lost love. Love, interrupted. "Straight" love. Rough love.

You'll find all of these in *Best Gay Romance 2012*, a spectrum of stories ranging in sexual intensity from sweetly romantic to hot-and-heavily lusty.

Most popular this year? Young love. Two boys in love bust open one boy's closet with musical passion, in Steve Berman's bubbly "Gomorrahs of the Deep, a Musical Coming Someday to Off-Broadway." Two schoolboys meet backstage at the theater, and the curtain rises on their romance, in Anthony McDonald's nostalgic "The Curtain Store." Two young cinephiles whose imaginations embrace different centuries find each other on the big screen, in Aaron Chan's charming "Cinema Love." Two twentysomething metalheads learn to make beautiful music together in Steve Isaak's cautious "Splatterdays." And two high school seniors transform a rocky friendship into boyhood romance in Martin Delacroix's dark "Cody Barton."

Love, unexpected: A rebel by day and a prince by night swoons into capitalist arms in Jamie Freeman's faaaabulous "Charming Princes." A man mourning his dead lover rekindles emotions after an encounter on the beach in Håkan Lindquist's moving "From a Journey."

Lost love: Two boyhood chums learn how much they love each other when one reaches out to the other from his grave, in Ron Radle's heartbreaking "To Brandon with Love, Justin." One man's memories of a lover departed are rekindled by the sight of two young men at play, in Simon Sheppard's reflective "Hello, Young Lovers."

Love, interrupted: Unattainable jock reunites with lovesick geek at a high school reunion and the tables are turned, in Rob Rosen's spunky "Prom King." Two men transcend the pain of their closeted military academy affair when they meet a decade later in C. C. Williams's pained "The Prisoner."

"Straight" love: Two hunks cast in a reality show for their testosterone-fueled masculinity vie for each other rather than for the Bachelorette in Gregory L. Norris's dick-heavy "The Bachelors."

Rough love: A Master loves his lad, with the aid of a whip, in Fyn Alexander's S/M-set "Precious Jade."

The heart finds many ways. Different intensities, yes, but these stories share the comfort of falling in love, of being in love, sometimes for a moment, sometimes for a lifetime.

Richard Labonté
Bowen Island

GOMORRAHS OF THE DEEP, A MUSICAL COMING SOMEDAY TO OFF-BROADWAY

Steve Berman

When I was seven, my babysitter sat me down on the plump couch in our basement and promised me an entire bowl of butter pecan ice cream if I would be quiet while she watched a DVD. I think she had a report due for class and had decided to rent the movie rather than read the book. As the opening credits ran for *Kiss Me, Kate* I stuffed spoonful after spoonful into my mouth. But by the time the cast sang "We Open in Venice" I had forgotten about the ice cream and stared wide-mouthed at the television. My legs began to swing with the music, upsetting the bowl. Melted, sticky goo spilled over both our laps.

That night my eyes opened to new wonders, my ears heard a new heartbeat. I began begging my parents to buy me that DVD, and others, too. My fairy tales were movies featuring Princes Charming like Danny Kaye and Gene Kelly. I didn't lack for ogres—such as Audrey II from *Little Shop of Horrors*—or wicked witches with appetites—for that, there was Lola from *Damn Yankees*.

Since then I have wished life were more like musicals. But people don't burst into song and dance when their emotions rise or fall. Mouthing lyrics while listening to your iPod or wailing in the shower while shampooing your hair don't count. I want a chorus to warn me of danger while singing verse. I want the romance of being serenaded, of the duet. And all I get is high school.

One night, my boyfriend asked me to come over to study. My hope was we'd be making out rather than struggling through *Moby Dick,* a book that squashed my brain like a lead weight whenever I tried to read more than a few pages. Then I saw what Hugh had done to his bedroom. Photocopies of thick-bearded old men had replaced the posters of Bob Dylan, Morrissey and the Red Caps.

"Herman Melville and Walt Whitman," he said, with the blatant ardor most gay boys reserve for pop stars thick with eye shadow or young actors infamous for stripping off their shirts on film.

"Like the bridge?" My experience with Whitman involved crossing the Delaware River from South Jersey into Philly so we could hit the Trocadero Theater to watch indie bands.

"Like *the* gay poet."

"Oh." I collapsed on his messy bed. I lay on my stomach and rested my chin on my hands. "So you like...really want to study?"

He nodded. "Remember, our oral presentations are due this week."

"Fine," I sighed. Being at the tail end of the alphabet, I had planned on procrastinating until Thursday. "Can we work out an incentive program? I'm thinking it's about time someone invented Strip Book Report."

Hugh raised an eyebrow. The left, which went a little wild near the center of his forehead. I wanted to pluck the few errant hairs while he slept. But it matches his mop of unruly curls.

"Not book reports...oral presentations—"

"Imagine. We take off our sneaks after writing the introductory sentence." I rolled over and dramatically kicked off one cherished Converse All-Star. "State our thesis, off come the shirts. By the time we're at the conclusion, the floor is covered with our clothes." I stretched my head back, off the side of the bed, and offered my best leer, seventeen years in the making.

He leaned over and kissed me. A bit sloppy, but that's fine because we both laughed. Then he shook his head. "No. I need to work on this."

"So I'm moral support. I can help you navigate Wikipedia for answers."

He clamped a hand over my mouth at that. "Heresy!" I stuck my tongue out and licked his palm, which doesn't taste that great but one has to know. No boyfriend was ever perfect.

"I have this *tremendous* idea."

When he took his hand away, I felt the beginning of a frown. Hugh's ideas, especially when he considers them *tremendous* or *monumental,* usually end up being problematic. Like last summer when he decided to rewrite Shakespeare's *Taming of the Shrew* as a webcomic featuring actual critters. I cured him by downloading the awful movie *The Killer Shrews* on my netbook and loudly playing clips whenever he mentioned the otter Petruchio falling for a furry Kate.

"Do tell."

"I'm going to do a whole presentation—not some sixth-grader's book report—on the homoeroticism in *Moby Dick.*"

I laughed. Awful move. Worse, I tell him: "You might as well sing it."

His expression grew pensive, then hurt. Like last summer when he went through a phase he called Inner Fat and wore nothing but baggy clothes. At one point, I pulled his boxers over his navel without giving him a wedgie and told him he was ridiculous. He sulked for nearly two weeks before I dragged him free of the bad mood by insisting he watch quirky French films with me.

"It's not a dumb idea."

I sat up in his bed. "I never said that. But even if there's some gay in the book—"

"There is. Lots. Whole scenes." He blinked at me, as if trying to wake from a bad dream. "Didn't you read it?"

"I'm more a SparkNotes kinda guy. But why would you want to rub their noses in it?"

"They're not puppies," he said.

I suddenly envisioned the students in Mr. Shimel's English class as dogs. Tracy Borland's thing for scrunchies earned her labradoodle status. Brian Coleman's jaw belonged to an English bulldog. When Derek Fiesler wore his basketball jersey—a glimpse of muscled arm and hairy pits!—that would be one hot Great Dane.

"Besides. I'm out. You're out."

"But neither of us wears pink shirts. We're like...assimilated. Why call so much attention to being different? Different is death in high school."

"I'm tired of acting like everyone else," he said. "We're not—"

"Maybe I am."

"You're not. You're a theater geek."

"I prefer thespian."

"You work stage crew."

"Ersatz thespian."

"You just used the word 'ersatz.' That's an SAT expression."

"Now a good vocab is being lavender, too?"

"Help me," he said.

I shook my head. "And feel all those fears from when I first came out rush back into my chest? No thanks." Even as I said that, my heartbeat raced faster, my stomach parkoured around my middle. I didn't even want to be in class if he was going to be writing G-A-Y on the whiteboard in front of everyone. I heard phantom laughter.

"Not with this." I grabbed my backpack, zipped up my hoodie and left his room; rushing down the stairs, I didn't even bother to call out a good-bye to his folks.

The suburban streets were quiet and cold, but my anger was keeping me warm. It was late November, but few houses on the block were lit because the neighborhood prefers menorahs to tinsel. I kept to the middle of the street. My hands were tucked away in the pocket of my white hoodie.

I soon heard my boyfriend's car whining behind me. When he rolled down the window, music from the radio filled the air.

Then he sang: *"Get in the car. It's cold. Don't be so angry all the time."*

I kept walking, but more slowly.

"Get in the car. Don't make me beg. Don't make me rhyme."

I stopped and turned. *"Don't call me Ishmael."*

"I won't." he said. "Your name is Greg."

I took a step forward, resting my hands on the open car window.

"Tell me you won't go through with this. Tell me that tomorrow will be sane."

He shook his head. *"I can't. I won't. Don't you see? That would go against my grain."*

"They'll laugh at you and, if I stand by you, me as well."

"What else does English class do than make our lives a hell?"

"It's only Melville."

"Only Melville?"

I kicked his car door, shouted, and walked away. *"Don't call me Ishmael!"*

He drove after me.

"You're afraid of what? That I'll make of fool of us? But I can't stay quiet anymore."

"It's just a book about a whale. Nothing else. You're finding fags where there aren't, all to start some stupid war."

"You saw the line. 'Bosom friends.' If that's not the gayest thing you ever heard a sailor say—"

I blinked into the glare of his headlights.

"I'm drawing a line. Right here and now on the street. Abandon please this Moby Dick essay.

It's only Melville."

He stopped the car and leaned his head out the window. *"Only Melville?"*

"Please," I sang. *"Don't call me Ishmael."*

He opened the driver's side door, singing right back:

"He had a voice. Like any of us, he wanted to be heard!"

"He's long since dead. Are you some literary nerd?"

"I won't put the man in the closet, like all the teachers do."

"He's better off in the dark. Find another book to review."

"Why won't you be my Ishmael, why won't you be my first mate? I need your strength for this effort, I need you to relate."

I stepped back from the car.

"I'm not some Ishmael, I am only a Gregory. You'll do this alone. I won't be part of some classroom...infamy."

And I ran all the way home.

* * *

The next day, during lunch, my best friend Casey lowered her vintage cat-eye glasses farther down her nose and then poked me with a french fry. "You look like someone took away your pixie sticks *and* your parents blocked Bravo."

"I had a fight with Hugh."

She dipped the offending fry into mayonnaise puddled atop a napkin on her lunch tray. "Not 'we had a fight.' So you admit this was all your fault?"

"Did not!"

"Well, what weren't you solely guilty of offending him with?"

"He wants to give a presentation in Shimel's class. On how gay Melville was."

"What's wrong with that?"

"It's crazy. Capital C crazy. The kids will tear him apart."

Casey rolled her eyes. "Please. You know how much of the assigned reading has a gay subtext? We're all used to it by now." She nudged Sharon, who was sitting beside her, causing her to spill milk down her chin. "Right? Some of us like reading about all that boy-smooching."

Casey stood on the bench and sang:

"If you squint real hard you'll actually see
great works of literature don't shy from sodomy."

My eyebrows rose. I glanced around but the rest of the cafeteria seemed ignorant that a senior wearing thrift store chic was singing in their midst. They only cared about their greasy carbs or wilted salads.

"It's all subtext I'll have you know,
of boys wanting to find some beau.

Read 'tween the lines if you don't believe me."

Then Sharon and the other girls sitting at our table lifted their lunch trays over their heads, swiveled around and swayed.

"And we girls, how we love to think of those guys
stranded on the beach in Lord of the Flies,
waiting for fair-haired Ralph to conquer his Jack,
while the choir boys 'round them didn't hold back."

Casey kicked away a foil-wrapped burger.

"Think fan-fic is only recently?
I'd wager folk in the sixteenth century
wanted that hunk Romeo
to dump Juliet for Mercutio.
Read 'tween the lines if you don't believe me."

The chorus of girls joined in:

"And we girls, how we love our gamecock.
That Watson adored his roomie Sherlock.
Sure Doyle gave the good doctor a wife.
But we all know Holmes was his fantasy life."

Casey leaned down and offered me a hand to step up onto the table. I shook my head no, so she grabbed my arm and pulled me up with surprising verve.

"Mark Twain's books aren't immune to such gaiety.
Or did you miss the crossdressin' Huckleberry?
Running off with his Jim

for reasons not so prim.
Read 'tween the lines if you don't believe me."

"You're crazy," I said. And looked down to see I had stepped in mac 'n' cheese. My poor Converses. Dairy and canvas don't match.

After cleaning off in the bathroom, I was late to algebra. Ms. Benress turned from the blackboard, already marked up with problems galore, to give me the stink-eye as I took my seat.

I began copying *x*'s and *y*'s in my notebook. Why anyone would ever want to add two such different numbers was beyond me. *X*'s were...well, like me. A bit naughty by nature (you never see moonshine jugs with YYY on them or hope to see a Y-rated movie). *X*'s were complicated. Like an intersection or a cross-roads. But passionate, especially with *O*'s. But Hugh was totally a Y. Always wondering about things. Y this? Y that? And yet... you couldn't spell so many wonderful words without Y. Dearly. Sweetly. Smartly. Yummy needed two.

Ms. Benress asked the class who would like to solve the latest equation she had chalked on to the board. Hands went up. Not mine. Yes, still she called on me. I groaned and slid out from behind my desk.

But my mind wasn't even attempting to do the algebra. Instead, it put words to the patter of my feet, the tapping of someone's pencil, even the ticking of the old clock on the wall.

"Answers aren't ever easy,
not when you're unsure you're right.
Not when you love him dearly,
perhaps I'm just too uptight?"

"The *X*'s and *Y*'s please," Ms. Benress said.

"X marks the spot of my heart.
Only one boy has the map.
If singing keeps us apart,
I'll end up feeling like crap.
How does he ever love me
when I only question Y?
What I've done, what misery.
Who wants to say good-bye?"

I dropped the chalk, I turned from the board and headed out the door. I knew that Hugh would be eating lunch and headed back toward the cafeteria.

A hall monitor looked up from his paperback. He held up a hand to stop me.

"Please let me make amends now.
I'll risk two days detention,
to tell him my solemn vow.
Please I need his attention."

The monitor teared up and nodded his assent.

I ran to the cafeteria doors, pushed them open and...

...everyone but Hugh in fifth period lunch stared at me. Not Hugh because he wasn't there.

"Sorry," I muttered.

I waited for him by his locker as the bell rang.

He offered me a weak smile, the sort that is armor for your feelings. I had never hugged him at school before. I wanted to now, right then and there, but hesitated. He opened the locker door between us. More armor.

"You didn't eat lunch?" I asked.

He shook his head. "No, I went to the library to work on my report."

"Maybe I can help?" I rubbed at his shoulder.

"You haven't even read the book."

I winced. "True. Well then, can I borrow your *Dick?*"

"What?"

"The Melville. I want to know what all the fuss is about."

He lightly rapped the back of his head against his locker door. "What happened to your copy? We were assigned the book a month ago—"

"That reminds me to ask Amazon for a refund. Super Save Shipping my ass."

"—and my presentation is today."

"Yes, but it's eighth period, last period of the day. I'll give it back before seventh. Promise."

"Fine." He handed it over.

I made sure to brush his fingers with mine when I took the book from him. He sighed, a sign—I hoped—that he was shedding some armor.

I brought the book with me to gym class. Yeah, Mr. Meno yelled at me, demanding I drop it, but I told him that the school board was far more concerned with me exercising my mind than my body. He growled a bit but ignored me for the rest of the class.

I could see that Melville liked his words, but I wasn't so much interested in what he wrote as I was following in the thread of notes that Hugh had made. They led me to one ongoing passage about Ishmael squeezing lumps of whale spermaceti—which I hoped wasn't what I thought it—*ugh*—with other crewhands. Hugh had written in tiny scrawl around the margins. I thought of secret codes and a thrill went through me:

Clearly this is Melville's attempt to show not only the joys of masturbation but how such an affectionate act can bring men closer.

I grinned and fought down a massive giggle. Hugh had written *masturbation.* Serious Hugh. I wondered if he got turned on while reading the passage, which seemed more gross than erotic to me.

Once the thirty minutes of chin-ups, push-ups and near throw-ups surrounding me were finished, I followed the other boys to the locker room, sat on the scarred wooden bench that ran down the middle of one tunnel of lockers and read more.

Before I had turned more than a couple of pages, though, I noticed that the usual accompanying din of guys changing and showering had…a rhythm?

I looked up from Melville to see a line of seniors, bare-skinned except for the towels wrapped around their waists, heading off to the showers. As they passed each locker, they slapped the metal door with their palms in a steady staccato, which they matched with a shanty:

"Yo, all young fellows that just might be queer
for me, way hey, blow the man down.
Best pay some attention and listen here.
Give me some time to blow the man down."

I set the book down on the bench and cautiously stepped to the end of the hall, watching the line of boys as each stripped off his towel and threw it onto a hook—every one landing with perfect precision—before they stepped under hissing showerheads.

"I'm a high school senior fresh from Jersey.
Breaking hearts because I have no mercy."

I edged closer. The testosterone in my blood reacting like iron fillings to a magnet. As the guys sang, they soaped themselves. The steam from the hot spray obscured...well, all the good parts, like a cartoon censor.

"When a cute guy is wanting a date
with me, way hey, blow the man down, when our bodies
touch that just might be fate.
Give me some time to blow the man down."

Each slick boy squeezed the soap in his hands—like the sailors of the *Pequod* had worked the spermaceti—causing the bars to leap into the air, only to be caught by the boy next in line. Not since I was seven had my jaw hung so low.

"Then tomorrow there'll be another boy
all while yesterday's one sheds tears ahoy.
You want me? Dare you take me home tonight?
For me, way hey, blow the man down
I'll leave your bedside, my exit stage right.
Give me some time to blow the man down."

I turned away from temptation...after a second look. I grabbed *Moby Dick* to shield the too-obvious effect of the shanty performance on my mainsail.

I ran into Hugh just before he walked inside his seventh-period class.

"Hey," he said.

My response was to tug him hard in the direction of the nearest boys' bathroom; he started to complain, but I told him French class could wait.

Once inside, I shoved him into a stall. I had a lot of enthusiasm to work out of my system.

He met my kisses with guarded measure. "But...I'll be...late."

My lips ate his words up. I slid one hand around to the back of his polo shirt, another hand to the front of his chinos.

He pressed his face into the crook of my neck and gasped. He managed to say, "Not here. Come over tonight. We'll watch *Les chansons d'amour* again."

My favorite film. "Promise?" We lost our virginity to Honoré's visuals and Beaupain's lyrics. I squeezed him tight as the echoes of the experience filled my head and chest.

"*Tu doives entendre je t'aime*," he said softly into my ear.

I stepped back. We chuckled at our obvious erections. His hand cupped my face for several seconds. Then we left the stall and sought to look more presentable.

"This is the greatest book ever," I said.

"Really?"

"No. But this may be the greatest day ever for me."

He kissed me again, on the cheek. "Don't be late for English. I'll need you there to cheer me on."

I decided, then, to skip study hall. I knew I had to do more than just applaud my boyfriend's efforts.

"Where did you get the guitar?" Hugh asked when he saw me sitting in the front row in English. For the first, and last, time.

"I borrowed it from the music department."

He smiled. "Do you even know how to play?"

"No, that's why I borrowed a guitarist, too." I waved toward Casey, who had cut class for a noble effort. "She owns every one of the Guitar Heroes."

When Mr. Shimel called Hugh to come up to the front of the class and begin his presentation, I followed.

"It's a duet," I told the heavy-set teacher.
Hugh cleared his throat.

"Ships are like prisons don't you know
men kept with other men on decks below.
Melville knew this from his life at sea,
he found homosexuality.
Let me tell you about the Gommorahs of the deep.
Let me tell you about the Gommorahs of the deep.
Proof's in Moby Dick, his most famous book.
Never were sailors so damn tight. Take a look."

Tracy Borland giggled, instigating an infection of chuckles and chortles that spread to the students around her. In response, I threaded my fingers between Hugh's to hold his hand tight. Then I pressed against Hugh, as if spooning him (which would happen tonight) as I sang the next verse.

"Think of that savage islander Queequeg.
In bed he harpooned Ishmael's pant leg.
What about that chapter where they all squeeze
out lumps of whale gunk, isn't that just a tease—"

Brian Coleman's wide mouth stopped masticating a lump of pinkish gum.
Hugh smiled.

"To boys like me, who search each book each day
for characters like me, proud to be gay."

Derek Fiesler grunted out "No way..." so it was only fair that I winked at him. His face flushed and he looked away.

"Ships are like prisons don't you know
men kept with other men on decks below.
Melville knew this from his life at sea,
he found homosexuality.
Let me tell you about the Gommorahs of the deep.
Let me tell you about the Gommorahs of the deep."

Then Hugh jumped back in:

"Melville wed, had a wife, that much is true.
But his real love was Hawthorne, a dude—
yes, that man who gave us The Scarlet Letter—
Melville's heart ached to know much better.
Before you say foul at what we have found
step wise and meet us on some common ground.
You, like us, like Melville, want only bliss
and that's why boys, when they want, should kiss."

In the moment of silence that followed, we kissed, right there, in front of the entire class. A kiss that lasted several moments as Casey geniused a guitar solo. I'd like to think we earned the B+ for that alone.

CHARMING PRINCES

Jamie Freeman

Our story began—as so many love stories do—with a shoe.

"Do you have this in size ten?" he asked the salesclerk. Her name tag identified her as Courtnei. A tiny heart-shaped sticker dotted the terminal letter.

Courtnei took the running shoe, turning it around in her hands, and said, "Do you want to see it in light blue too?"

"Sure." His smile was picture-perfect.

"Are you gonna buy those?" I asked.

He looked at me for the first time and my stomach lurched. He was beautiful in a way that made me look around to see if he was being filmed. A man this gorgeous could have stepped off a movie set, with his faded jeans and white Oxford shirt, perfectly manicured hands, Rolex, signet ring and expensively messy haircut. He had that fresh, sharply defined quality a man can only achieve through the consistent use of staggeringly over-priced skin-care products. Everything about him whispered: *wealth*. I looked into his pale-blue eyes, acutely aware of my tattered Levi's, stained T-shirt and army surplus jacket. I pointed to the poster I'd been clutching in front of me.

"Yes," he said.

I snorted in exasperation. Of course this child of privilege wouldn't get it.

"This woman works in a Honduran sweatshop making the shoes you're considering buying. She is paid less than twenty dollars a week despite the long hours and high productivity demands. She has no protection if she or one of her three children becomes ill. She is the sole support of her—"

"What's her name?"

"What?"

"I asked her name," he said. "Sometimes personalizing the message, say, something like, 'This is Maria Cortez. She works in a sweatshop near La Ceiba—'"

"Are you making fun of people in poverty?"

"No. I'm making fun of you." He smiled again, his lips parting in a frankly sensual manner.

"Okay, so I've got these in dark blue in ten and a half, and the light blue ones in ten." Courtnei pushed past me with a pair of shoeboxes. "He can't be here," she said to him, and then turned to me. "You can't be here."

"He's here with me," the man said.

"But he can't—"

"Thank you, Courtnei," the man said. "May I have a few minutes to talk with my friend? Then I'll try these on?"

"I'm not your friend," I said.

He shrugged. Courtnei looked dubious but drifted away.

"So you're here to keep people from buying these shoes?" he asked.

"Yes. The workers—"

"Wait." He held up his hand, the palm pink and perfect. The

gesture was strangely erotic. I shifted in place; he smiled again.

"You're still laughing at me."

"There is a difference between a smile and a laugh...and you need to tell me your name."

"I need to what?"

"Tell me your name."

I crossed me arms and considered my options.

"I'm Fletcher Alden," he said. He held out his hand. I shook it, feeling small and disoriented.

"Ashe," I said. "Ashe Stern."

He smiled again, blue eyes probing me. Sweat trickled down my back.

"You know, Ashe, in a country in which nearly forty percent of the population is unemployed or underemployed and seventy percent live in poverty, the fact that this company provides over five hundred jobs, on-site medical care, and wages that are fifty percent more than the federally mandated minimum wage could be seen as a good thing."

"Who're you supposed to be? Jeffrey Sachs?"

"No. I'm just saying this may be more complicated than it seems."

"That's a bullshit excuse."

"Most things are," he said.

"Are what?"

"More complicated than they seem."

"No," I said. I was trying unsuccessfully to work up some emotion about the Honduran workers, but all I could see was dark hair that tufted from the collar of Fletcher's bright white undershirt, the ample denim bulge between his legs and the heavily muscled runner's thighs that stretched the legs of his jeans. "This is about...this is about a definition of social justice that transcends national borders."

"As you say. You're clearly the expert."

I flushed.

"Do you believe that?" I asked.

"What? That you're an expert?"

"No. The other part, about the workers being better off."

He shook his head. "Not really. These shoes cost about seven dollars to produce, package and ship. They're on sale for a hundred and fifty. Somebody's making a bundle and I'm guessing it's not Maria Cortez, and because Courtnei works for minimum wage plus commissions, I doubt it's her either."

I hadn't really considered Courtnei's wages.

"Do you think she has health insurance?"

"Courtnei? Probably can't afford it."

"I hate this," I said.

"Then why are you here?"

"For Maria," I said.

"Don't you mean Courtnei?" he asked.

I sighed.

"Just yanking your chain," he said. "Courtnei? I'm going to pass on these."

"You're not gonna buy them?"

"No."

I blushed in confusion, unable to figure out if this was a victory. I dropped my eyes, studying my own fair-trade shoes, letting my brown hair fall down in front of my face, screening me from further scrutiny.

"So Ashe, after fighting the good fight all morning, you must be hungry."

"Are you asking me to lunch?" I asked.

"I'm pretty sure I am." Fletcher shifted his body into a cool, elegant pose. I watched the way he canted his hips and let his shoulders rise. It was a supremely natural movement, but it radiated sexiness and surety. I tried to create a quick mental note of it, wondering if I could recreate it onstage.

"Um?" I lost my train of thought somewhere between his hips and his shoulders.

"What would Maria Cortez say to the voice of the people having lunch with a prince of the merchant class?"

"You're not funny," I said, smiling slightly.

"I have my moments," he said. "And I'm getting hungry." His voice dropped into the gutter with that last word, but the inflection was so precise, so polished, that I wondered if I had heard correctly.

"So, lunch?" I said.

"Or something," he said.

He was standing closer to me suddenly, his warm body radiating the smell of clean sweat and sandalwood, the bulge in his jeans slowly becoming larger and more distinct.

He saw me glancing down at him and licked his lips. Again the gesture was subtle, could easily have been something else, but I saw the look in his eyes and knew he was toying with me. I liked it.

We left the store and cut over to Eighth Avenue, ambling uptown to the door of a little Italian bistro. The staff greeted Fletcher by name, ushering us past a crush of waiting tourists to an intimate table near the piano. The owner brought over a bottle of expensive Chianti and chatted amiably with Fletcher, asking in her throaty, sexy Italian accent about his mother and his sister; asking who I was, where we'd met and if this was a date. She clucked and laughed and winked at me, her wine-red fingernails clicking against the bottle as she poured a tasting portion for Fletcher.

When she was gone, Fletcher raised his glass. "To happy beginnings," he said. We clicked glasses and I sipped the smooth, dark wine.

Lunch was like a clever, funny romantic comedy montage scored by the tinkling ivory sounds of Arlen, Berlin and Gershwin. I'm sure we talked about all the boring things people find so fascinating when the chemistry is explosive, but I don't really remember any of it. I know we didn't talk about jobs or apartments, but Fletcher insists we traded family histories and coming out stories. I remember arguing over the check—I proposed we split it; he insisted on paying—and I remember watching him across the table throughout lunch and falling for him: for his pale, glowing skin and his perfect, lilting voice and his laugh, that perfect combination of deep, sexy rumble and high delighted peal. When we finally stood to leave, I didn't want to part from him.

After lunch, we stepped out onto the sidewalk, trying to hang on to the warm cozy feeling of the restaurant despite the honking, shoving crush of rush hour. It was a Monday afternoon; I didn't have to work that night, but I was still unsure of myself so I stood holding my backpack strap in one hand and laughing nervously.

"God, I'd like to have a go at those lips," he said finally.

"So what's stopping you?"

He grinned and blushed. He took a half step back and then, realizing what he'd done, stepped closer to me. We could almost pretend that the rush of people along the sidewalk was forcing us together. I could feel the heat of his body, smell his cologne. He laughed again and I leaned forward, planting a kiss on his beautiful, full lips, surprising us both. He leaned into the kiss, but softly, melting in my direction rather than taking a step. The kiss lasted an instant, but when I pulled back and opened my eyes I could see the heat in his.

"Oh, fuck it," he said, grabbing my elbow and yanking me into the flow of pedestrian traffic. He glanced over his shoulder and pulled me down the next street, heading back toward Times Square.

"Where are we going?"

"Someplace private." He looked over my shoulder again, pulled me across the street between a pair of tour buses, through a group of Asian tourists and into a Starbucks, then out the back door of the Starbucks and into the lobby of a hotel. We caught an elevator and he pressed the UP button, taking my hand in his and kissing my knuckles. The older straight couple with whom we shared the elevator seemed unfazed. I stepped closer to him, drawing his scent deep into my lungs. The elevator chimed and he pulled me through the door with him. I trailed along behind him through a conference center teeming with people in expensive suits.

"I take it you've been here before?" I asked.

"Yeah," he said.

"Um, where are we going?"

He looked over his shoulder with that dazzling grin of his. "Play with me, baby," he said. And he pulled me down a short corridor into a secluded restroom.

Three urinals faced three fully enclosed cubicles.

"Wait a minute." I stopped in my tracks.

"What?"

"A bathroom?" I said. "Really?"

"It's secluded."

"It's a bathroom."

"It's clean and the door goes all the way to the floor."

I stood watching him. He didn't grow impatient; he just stared at me hungrily and waited. I could see the bulge in his jeans shifting as blood rushed to his growing erection.

"C'mon," he said. "You're a rebel, Ashe."

"I'm a rebel?"

"Voice of the people, scourge of corporate America."

"You dragged me in here to make fun of me?" I laughed nervously.

"I dragged you in here to ravage you away from the prying eyes of the city."

I reached out and slid my palm along the length of his erection, feeling the heat beneath the tight denim. My own cock leapt to attention.

"So, do you come here often?" I asked.

"Ugh. You're killin' me," he said. "Get in here. C'mon, before somebody comes in. Come kiss me."

He opened the door and tugged me into the cubicle.

"What are we going to tell our grandchildren?" I asked as he closed and locked the door behind us.

"We'll tell them it started with a shoe."

"There's always a shoe," I said, turning to face him.

"And a charming prince," he said.

I blushed.

He lifted my backpack off my shoulder, hung it on the hook behind me and pulled me roughly against him. Our chests touched for the first time and I realized his body was hard and perfect beneath the flawless white cotton. I pushed closer, trying to make as much contact as possible and we kissed, not the soft, public kiss we'd shared on Eighth Avenue, but a full, insistent kiss that felt like an erotic eating contest.

His hands fumbled with my belt buckle and then my jeans and in an instant his long cool fingers were sliding along the length of my cock. He pushed my jeans down past my hips and held my cock in his hands, thumbing the slit to harvest a tiny pearl of precum. He raised his hand, looking intently at the viscous liquid and then smearing it across my lips. I shivered and he laughed that gentle, sexy laugh.

I pulled him close for another kiss, my cock sliding insistently against the front of his jeans. I unbuttoned his Oxford and pushed his T-shirt up, revealing planes of lightly furred muscles. We were kissing and rubbing our erections against each other, laughing, breathing heavy and making a lot of noise when there was a loud knock on the cubicle door.

We froze. His face went pale.

Another knock: five loud raps and then silence.

"Occupied," I said.

Fletcher stifled a snort of laughter.

"No shit, kid. This is hotel security. Get the fuck outta here or I'm calling the police. You got thirty seconds to beat it." I held my breath and listened to his footsteps as he walked across the tile floor and stepped through the door onto the carpet beyond.

"*Shit!*" My heart was trying to pound its way through my rib cage. My whole body jumped to life, the adrenaline spike so intense I felt like the Six Million Dollar Man. I was ready to outrun anyone.

"What are you doing?" Fletcher asked.

"What?"

"You're making that sound," he said, "and moving in slow motion or whatever?"

"Bionics," I said. "*Duh-nuh-nuh-nuh-nuh.*"

He rolled his eyes. "Well, come on, Steve Austin, let's get out of here."

When we pushed through the restroom door there was nobody in sight, but when we fast-walked through the hotel lobby, a trio of guys in burgundy jackets and matching Bluetooths appeared out of nowhere and started following us. Fletcher grabbed my hand, pulling me out onto the street and hailing a cab. He shoved me inside and dove in after me. We were halfway down the block and the three security guards were still standing in the street watching us.

"Where do you live?" he asked.

I hesitated. I lived in a tiny one-bedroom apartment with a roommate. I looked down at his perfect hands jutting from perfectly ironed, spotless white cuffs, and I froze, embarrassed and undecided about what to do next.

"What's the matter?" he asked. He touched my cheek. "It's okay."

I shook my head, changing the subject. "That was intense."

"Yeah, I guess so. Sorry. I never thought..." His voice trailed off.

He slid close to me and kissed me gently on the lips, his fingers gliding along my thigh and gently kneading the life back into my cock.

I gave the driver the cross streets.

My roommate, Bayani, was gone when we got to the apartment, so I dragged Fletcher into the tiny bedroom and locked the door behind us. He looked around, reading the titles of the books lined up on the shelves, scanning the posters and flyers that cluttered the walls on my half of the room.

"Street theater, political causes, boycotts, 'Fight Corporate Domination,' and this..." He pointed to a poster for the Disney production of *Cinderella* at the New Amsterdam.

"It's Rogers and Hammerstein," I said.

"Big Broadway is big business," he said.

"I should boycott art because it's corporately produced?"

He pointed to a bumper sticker tacked up over my desk. "You're boycotting NBC because it's owned by a defense contractor."

"Disney isn't a defense contractor."

There was an awkward moment of silence. He looked at me and winked. "It's okay. I'm just learning about you," he said. "And playing with you a little."

"Come play over here," I whispered.

"I'm almost done here," he said.

I dropped my backpack on the floor, kicked off my shoes and sat on my bed watching him.

"I love that you're so passionate about what you believe," he said. "These political causes and the incident in the shoe store; I like that a lot."

"Thanks?"

He turned around to face me. "I've never really been very politically active. I leave that to my father, or the family attorneys, you know; I never get too involved in anything."

"Not in anything at all?"

He smiled again. "Well, some things warrant involvement."

"So come get involved," I said. "*Now!*"

He chuckled, kicked off his shoes and stood at the edge of the bed looking at me.

"Sorry about the hotel thing," he said. "That was stupid."

"Nah. It's okay, I—"

"C'mere." He didn't wait for me to respond, he just pulled me over to the edge of the bed and started yanking my shirt up over my head. He stripped me out of my clothes and then slowly, his eyes never leaving mine, took off his own clothes. He was gym-toned and perfect, his chest and legs covered in dark, closely manicured fur. His body tapered from broad, muscular shoulders to ribs and rippling abs in a perfect V-shape.

I pulled him on top of me and we rolled around for a while, kissing and exploring each other. His cock was long and straight with an intimidatingly large head that left streaks of shimmery precum on my legs, my stomach and my cheeks. The heady saltiness of his skin made me want to take a bite out of him.

He rolled on top of me, spreading my arms above my head and pinning me to the mattress. "Don't move," he whispered, sliding his tongue inside my ear and sending a shiver down the length of my body. A dimpled landscape of goose bumps appeared across my arms and legs.

He kissed and licked his way down the side of my face and neck, and then wandered toward my left armpit. When his tongue touched the delicate skin under my arm, my body jerked involuntarily.

"Jerking away will send me away for a while, but I always come back for what I want," he said.

"I'll remember that," I said, gasping as his teeth clamped down on my nipple.

"Please do," he murmured.

He traced the contours of my body like an intimate cartographer while I shifted and quaked beneath his lips.

When I could stand it no longer, I told him to get condoms and lube out of the desk drawer. He pulled the pale-green condom down over my cock, lubed us both up and straddled me. I watched his face crinkle and relax as he worked my cock inside him; sweat beaded on his forehead. He let out a long, breathy sigh as he finally settled onto me, sliding down to the root and reaching forward to kiss me again. He took charge from the top, moving until he found a rhythm that suited him and then looking down into my eyes and coaxing me forward with him. His six-pack abs rippled beneath the taut skin; his breath was heavy, rising sometimes into moans that shook his body and tightened all of his internal muscles. I was sweating beneath him, coaxed into a delirium of sensation, and just when I thought I might pass out from the strain, I felt hot blasts of cum splashing onto my chest, neck and face. I tilted my head, letting the cum fall onto my lips and tongue. The taste of him sent me over the edge. I leaned forward, pulling him against me and pumping everything I had into his body. I groaned and felt tears mingling with the sweat on my cheeks.

* * *

Later, when I opened my eyes, he was still lying on top of me, his face inches from my own. I lifted myself on one elbow, shifting our bodies and looking down at him. His eyes opened, slowly gaining focus. There was a moment of stillness and then he kissed me so passionately I collapsed back on the bed, his body still glued to mine. My cock slid out of him. He reached down to drop the condom on the floor beside the bed without breaking the kiss.

We kissed for a long time, through the heat and exhaustion, his body melding itself to mine. I reached to pull a blanket over the two of us as his lips fluttered against my neck. I didn't ask him at the time, but later Fletcher told me he kept saying, "This is the one, this is the one" over and over until he drifted off to sleep.

We were awakened by Bayani banging on the bedroom door.

"Occupied," Fletcher said.

I laughed and then covered my mouth with my fingers.

"What the fuck? Ashe, let me in."

We scrambled into our clothes; Fletcher disposed of the condom and I opened the door.

"Oh, Jesus, Ashe, it smells like a sex club in here." Bayani stormed into the room wearing lace-up Daisy Dukes, knee-high Doc Martens and glitter. He pushed past me without seeming to notice Fletcher. He dropped to his knees and started pulling wads of clothing from under his bed.

"This is Fletcher."

"Hey, Fletch." He didn't turn around. "What are you still doing here? We've got, like ten minutes to get to the theater."

I glanced at Fletcher.

"Dude, today's Monday," I said.

"Seriously?" Bayani looked genuinely startled.

"You're in a play?" Fletcher asked.

Bayani laughed. "Are you kidding me? He's—"

I hit him in the face with a pillow.

"What? Is it some kind of embarrassing guerrilla theater? Anticorporate flash mobs or something? Hassling the shoppers in the Disney Store?"

I'm sure Fletcher was being sincere, but this sent Bayani to the floor, laughing and rolling back and forth, then beating his heels on the floor, tears seeping from the corners of his eyes. He was only a moderately talented actor, so I was pretty sure the tears were real.

"What?" Fletcher said again.

"Disney!" Bayani hooted and collapsed again, laughing and on the verge of hysteria.

"What?" Fletcher turned to me.

I didn't say anything, but Bayani rolled onto his back, panting. "He's fucking Prince Charming," he said. "You know? In *Cinderella?* At the New Amsterdam," Bayani said, hooting with laughter. "It's a Disney show. Flash mobs! Fuckin' guerrilla theater."

Fletcher's eyes widened perceptibly but he didn't say anything.

Bayani was staggering to his knees, saying something about *Tarzan* being the only Disney show he'd ever heard of with gorillas.

"Come on, man. It's not that funny," I said.

This resulted in another round of panting and giggling.

"Can you give us a minute, B?"

Bayani pulled on a purple rain slicker and stalked into the other room.

"Disney isn't a defense contractor," Fletcher said, his tone gentle but mocking.

I couldn't read his face, but it didn't really matter; I was so embarrassed I wanted to die.

"You protest people buying those shoes when you work across the street in a show that charges five hundred dollars for front-row tickets?"

"It's not the same thing," I said.

"Isn't it?" I still couldn't read his face. There was something there that wasn't there before, something that looked dark, maybe angry. "Disney is not a defense contractor, but they own ABC and they use the media to shape American public policy; they fight American unions tooth and nail; they rely on under-paid foreign labor for their production base.... I could go on."

"Please don't."

We stared at each other for a moment in silence.

"I thought this meant something to you," he said, pointing to the protest posters on the wall.

I heard my father's voice in his words. Old wounds reopened and tears welled in my eyes.

"Maybe this was a bad idea," I said.

"What?" He seemed genuinely surprised.

"Maybe I'm not what you think I am."

"Don't say that. It doesn't—"

"I think you should go," I said.

"Ashe, no—"

"Just go, Fletcher."

"You're a fucking idiot," Bayani said, when Fletcher was gone.

"Can you just shut the fuck up? Quit your giggling and laughing and stay the fuck out of my life just this once?" I screamed, grabbing my jacket and storming out the door. I took the service elevator and went out through the back alley, heading uptown toward the park.

I was so full of angry energy that I broke into a run, sprinting as far as Columbus Circle, letting sweat and heat loosen my joints and clear my head. I crossed into the park and plotted a rambling course toward the Bethesda Fountain.

Embarrassment was thick inside me, viscous and hot and acidic.

An actor? A lousy fuckin' actor? Jesus, Ashe, I thought your political beliefs meant something to you. My father's disapproval echoed in Fletcher's words; they both thought I was a complete sellout. And wasn't I?

I stormed through the darkening park, sometimes walking, sometimes running, always trying to keep a few paces ahead of the choking shame. I was running when I passed the reservoir and staggering by the time I reached Central Park North. I collapsed on a bench, breathless and exhausted, a wreck of wounded pride. I hated myself so much I considered throwing myself in front of the Number Three bus. I imagined the scrape of asphalt on my face and the crunching progress of the tires across my back and legs. It took me an hour to calm down, but as my anger and embarrassment ebbed, a rising tide of despair washed over me.

What the fuck had I done? Had I just sent a gorgeous, funny, smart, rich man packing because of my wounded pride?

I called Bayani on my cell.

"I don't know what to do," I said.

"Have you considered throwing yourself in the river?"

"I was thinking of a launching myself under the tires of a crosstown bus."

"Right. And then I'll be stuck pushing your crippled ass around in a wheelchair—*But ya are, Blanche! Ya are in that chair!*" He broke into peals of laughter.

"Not funny," I said.

"You know I'm funny, bitch," he said.

"I'm sorry about before," I said.

He sighed loudly, and then said: "You white boys are so dramatic. Just call him."

I smiled.

Until I realized I had absolutely no way of contacting Fletcher.

My grandmother used to say, "Pride goeth before a fall."

I always hated the crazy old bat.

I went back to work the next day, stumbling through the week in a half-dazed stupor that would have gotten me fired if it weren't for the persistent and skillful intervention of the company's Equity steward, Bambi. But even she was getting tired of my lackluster performances by the end of the week. She pulled me aside before the Sunday evening show and whispered in my ear: "You quit fucking up or I'm letting you tank. You got your week; now get your shit together."

I caked on makeup to cover the bags under my eyes and tried not to cry during the love songs. The Sunday evening performance was a significant improvement. Bambi stopped me in the hall after curtain, grabbed my arms and said, "Better. Now go home, sleep until Tuesday afternoon, and come back in here reborn. You got it, Ashe?" I nodded and slinked away.

Bayani was waiting for me in the hallway in his street clothes.

"There's a package back there for you." He jerked his head in the direction of my dressing room.

"My walking papers?" I asked.

"I'm thinking, no," he said.

There was a rectangular package wrapped in royal purple with an extravagant blue ribbon. There was a card tucked under the bow. I pulled out the envelope with trembling fingers and read the note.

> *Best show all week. If the shoe doesn't fit, the shop's open 'til midnight—Fletcher.*

I pulled the top off the box, revealing a pair of the blue running shoes Fletcher had not bought at the shoe store on the day we met.

I arrived at the store at ten minutes to midnight. The place was packed with tourists scooping up last-minute deals to take home to Scranton or Cleveland or Baltimore.

I had the box tucked under one arm and I was looking for Fletcher. Courtnei approached me and said, "Can I help you?"

"Yes, I'd like to return these," I said.

"Oh, it's *you.* Where's your protest sign?"

"I retired the sign."

"Change of heart?"

"You could say that."

"Did you steal these?"

"No."

"Do you have the receipt?"

"I've got it," a voice said from behind me.

I turned around. Fletcher was wearing jeans and a tight white T-shirt. In the very center of his chest, nestled in the gentle slope between his pecs, was a cartoon frog wearing a jeweled crown.

I handed the box to Courtnei without looking at her. Fletcher handed her the receipt, took me in his arms and kissed me.

We came up for air when Courtnei nudged Fletcher with a clipboard. He scrawled his signature on the return slip and handed her his American Express Black card.

"Should I expect drama every time I uncover an inconsistency in your character?" he asked.

"Probably," I said. "Does that scare you?"

"I guess not. How many can there possibly be?"

"There are a lot of them, I'm afraid."

"So it could take years to work through them all."

"Decades, maybe."

"It sounds exhausting."

"Oh, I'll definitely exhaust you."

"I don't doubt that for a minute." He said. "And the drama?"

"I *am* an actor," I said. "A master thespian, you might say."

"Oh, I wouldn't say that. Not *this* week anyway," he said, laughing.

I dug my knuckles into his rib cage.

"You came to the show?"

"Seven times."

"You missed one?"

"It was a matinee."

"Still..."

"I have a life," he said.

"Got any pointers for me?" I asked.

"Yeah, try reining it in a little when you do that thing you do with your left hand. You know, the thing with the flick and the bow and the kiss." He demonstrated, exaggerating my flourish, making it look outrageously effeminate. "I mean, you're kissing Cinderella, not Lady Gaga."

"I worked hard on that move," I said, but I was laughing.

"Right."

"You didn't like it?"

"Kinda gay."

"Ya think?" I slid my hand across his chest, tweaking his

right nipple through the tight cotton.

"Oh, yeah," he said. "Way gay."

"Any other notes?" I asked.

"Don't run away from me." He put his hands on my arms, suddenly serious.

"Never again."

"Never again," he said. "Because I'll just follow you."

"There's no escaping a happy ending," I said.

The overhead lights flashed and the manager made an announcement that the store would be closing in three minutes.

Fletcher wrapped his arm around my waist and pulled me close, kissing me hard on the mouth, recreating in exact detail the final kiss from the show.

"And curtain," he whispered, his lips warm against my cheek.

TO BRANDON WITH LOVE, JUSTIN

Ron Radle

Me and Justin Thulon grew up together in a little town called
Bolt, Texas, about thirty miles outside Arlington. Little ol' place.
I mean, there couldn't been more than five hundred or so people
lived there (and it ain't done nothing but shrink ever since then).
Me and Justin were next-door neighbors, so it was natural we
took up with each other. Beginning at nine years old we were
buddies and did everything together. Went fishing. Rode four
wheelers. Played little league football and baseball, too. But
we liked fishing the best. It was a way to get away from other
folks and be to ourselves and talk about things or just not say
anything at all and enjoy *that*.

But it didn't last for long. Well, not long enough. When I was
twelve my daddy announced we were moving to South Carolina
because he was taking a new job. He had family there too. In
fact that's where his mama and daddy were living at the time,
so we would be moving close to them. Daddy said he had found
a job there on purpose because he wanted to get back close

with his mama and daddy. They were getting older and were not in the best of health, and they needed him. Well, I didn't have anything against that. But I sure didn't want to leave Bolt, because leaving Bolt meant leaving Justin Thulon, and I couldn't stand the thought of that. I even asked Daddy if there wasn't any way I could stay in Bolt and live with Justin and his mama and daddy, but Daddy shook his head firm in response. No way. I had to go to South Carolina with them. So I went.

But I didn't like it. I cried and cried all the way out there—I was a twelve-year-old boy just sniveling and going on so much my mama turned around and threatened to whup the tar out of me right there in the car. But all I could think of was Justin and our good times together. Man, you should have seen how far me and him could jump them gullies on the four-wheelers, and us little fellows and all! We'd fly like birds and just scare the yellow tee-tee right out of our poor mamas. There was the fishing. The sports. The jokes we played on girls with rubber snakes and plastic lizards. The way at night we'd lie under the great big Texas sky and make patterns out of the stars with our fingers. We'd decided we were brothers in a way, not blood brothers, but brothers of the heart and spirit, although I am not sure that's the way we worded it back then. But it was the way we meant it. And we vowed always to be buddies and brothers, and then, durned if my daddy didn't go and get that job in South Carolina and make me be the one to break our promise.

Well, the years passed in South Carolina. I got used to things. Me and Justin talked on the phone and sent emails and text messages and such, and then all of a sudden communication quit between us. I got involved in high school football and baseball; I dated girls; just the usual stuff in teen years. And I reckon Justin did the same. And when you get busy it's awfully easy to lose touch with people, even your best friend and brother of the heart and soul. That's what happened, and pretty soon I turned eighteen and was out of high school and in college. I attended a small community college in town but had plans to go to the big school in Columbia eventually.

So everything was settled or seemed to be. Then something happened to turn it all upside down.

One day in spring I was leaving my statistics class, headed for my car, when who do you reckon comes roaring into the school parking lot on his big Harley-Davidson but Justin Thulon? That's right. He came in with a roar, doing wheelies and turning that hog round and round so everyone would see him. That was his style. Show-offy. Grand. Big. Just like you'd expect of somebody from Texas. He landed that monster right at my feet and through his black Ray-Bans, said to me, "What's happenin', partner?"

"What's happenin' with *you*, you crazy sumbitch?" I asked him and just laughed, 'cause he was there, in South Carolina, and 'cause of the way he had made his entrance. Just classic Justin.

"I'll have you know, buster boy," he answered me, "that I am now a resident of the state of South Carolina. Yes, sir. I done knocked off the Texas dust from my heels, and I am now a Carolinian!"

Well, that just all seemed too crazy to me. I needed an explanation. He told me to get on back of him, and I did, and he roared us out of that parking lot and cut up and down main streets and side streets until we came to an apartment complex just a little ways out from downtown, a brick place with two stories and cement columns and cement steps. He cut off the engine of his hog and held out his arm in a dramatic way. "That's my residence now, Brandon Bobo. That's my abode. My castle."

"What the hell, Justin? And how?"

He led me up the steps to his apartment and into the place, which had some unopened boxes on the floor and such. He was still unpacking. He closed the door and held out his arms again, this time to receive me in them. I went to him. We hugged big and long. I stepped back. In all the crazy confusion of his arrival, I hadn't noticed the physical change in Justin. I mean he was *buff*! My eyeballs just bulged out at how muscular he had gotten. When we were growing up and all, Justin had always been skinny and had stayed that way up to the time I left Texas. Now he had big shoulders and a wide chest and guns with healthy looking veins. This was all apparent through his blue T-shirt and the black leather vest over it. He had grown him a little goatee too to go along with his moustache, and he kept his light brown hair cut short, almost military style but not quite a buzz cut. All in all, he was pretty impressive.

"You've turned into Superman, ain't you? Where'd you get all them muscles, boy? You just rentin' them or what?"

He laughed. "Rent to own. They're mine. Hit the gym when I turned fifteen. Been at it ever since. This is the result." He made a muscle with one arm so the bicep stood up, hard and meaty.

"You a stud now!" I told him, and that made him laugh again.

"Damn right!"

We cleared space off the couch. His folks had come with him from Bolt with a U-Haul to help him move. He said he just decided he wanted to be back close to me, that he missed me, that he was tired of Texas, and he was old enough to decide if he wanted to make the move. His mama and daddy weren't thrilled about him wanting to move so far away, but what could they say? He was eighteen. A legal adult. He didn't have a job yet, but he was scouring the want ads. Did I know of anything? I told him I had a work-study job at the school helping out in one of the administrative offices. He wanted to know if I could get him one. I laughed and told him he had to be enrolled in school first before he could apply. That made him frown, which made me laugh again. Justin was no fan of higher education. He was lucky, he said, to have gotten a high school diploma.

Our talk went on like that for a while. I asked him if he had left a girlfriend behind in Bolt, and he said no, he hadn't been seeing anybody steady. "Just playin' the field." I told him it was the same for me, that I had other things on my mind right then, and other goals. We wound up back at the college to get my car, and then we went over to this Mexican restaurant in town for supper. It was nothing like the TexMex you could get in Arlington, but it wasn't bad. I had the enchiladas rancheros, and Justin had a plate of steak fajitas. When we got done with supper we stopped by the house, so Mama and Daddy could see Justin, and they were just as shocked and happy as I was that he had moved to South Carolina. It was late by the time all the talk was through, and Justin was heading out the door for his apartment when he stopped me at the door and whispered, "Why don't you move out of here and in with me? There's room. And you're old enough to be on your own, don't you think?"

It was a thought, one I turned over and over in my head in bed that night and one that kept me from getting a good night's sleep. But that wasn't the only thing. I couldn't get over how good Justin looked, just popping out with muscles and everything. Another thought occurred to me right out of nowhere, one I hadn't been looking for that surprised me: I would have loved to have seen the shape of Justin's muscles outside of his clothes. Naked. Head to foot. Wow, that idea just knocked the breath out of me. Where had it come from? I tried to shoo it away and go to sleep, but I couldn't. In fact, the desire got more and more dirty. I could see Justin not only naked but touching himself. Yeah. One hand was squeezing one of his nipples, pinching the tip, and the other had hold of his dick, and he was giving it a good, hard jerking too, making his whole body shake and his face bunch up in concentration, just like the dudes do in the porno flicks. And pretty soon he was emptying his load into the air, just spurting white juice all over the place. Again I tried to get the image out of my head. And I found myself just soaking wet, man—I mean, just hot from head to foot, and drenched. Had the fantasy of my buddy pulling his pud got me into such a state? That worried me.

I got out of bed and went to the window and stared out at the dark. Didn't think of anything. Didn't want to. But my hands thought for me. They unbuttoned my pajama top, whipped it away from my arms and let it drop to the ground. Then they went for the bottoms. Pulled 'em away from my hips, pushed them down my legs, until I was at the window stark naked, or almost. Then it occurred to me how close Justin was: just a few miles away, not hundreds or even a thousand. He was right across town in his new apartment, probably as naked as me. My hands found my dick hard and standing straight up, touching the windowsill. I moved some till the head ran into the window itself, and I began to rub it back and forth. I was tracing Justin's name into the windowpane. I grabbed hold of my dick, and a wave of tingly heat shimmered over my skin. I closed my eyes and thought of me and Justin together like this, naked, coming close, each taking the other into his arms, embracing, running our hands over each other's bare skin, arms, chest, bare butt. The image got me so excited I jerked my dick the way I'd pictured Justin jerking his, going at it real hard, playing with my tits the way he had in my fantasy, moaning, until I couldn't take it anymore, and the white stuff just hopped out of me and hit the windowpane, *one, two, three* shots of it, big globs running down the glass. When the good feeling had passed and I was calm again, I took my dick and smeared it in the goo, again trying to write Justin's name.

Mama and Daddy weren't crazy about the idea of me moving in with Justin. I didn't think they would be. They loved Justin and all, but they knew he wasn't the most responsible human being in the world. Too fun-loving. They worried he might not get a job and would stick me with the bills while he just played around. I told them I thought he had changed, even though I didn't have one bit of proof of such a thing. It was just that I wanted to live with Justin, to be as close to him as possible, and I didn't really need their permission. I was over eighteen. Still, I wanted them to approve. I told them that I'd look out for myself. I wouldn't let Justin or anybody else hoodoo me.

But after I settled in with Justin, I wondered if they didn't have a point, because Justin sure didn't seem in any kind of hurry to get a job. Oh, he didn't bum money off me or anything. He seemed to have his own cash. I'm not sure where he got it, but he paid his share of the rent and the utilities. I was just worried that money, wherever it came from, might run out in a hurry. The bulk of it he spent in socializing. He wasn't twenty-one yet, but that didn't stop him from going out to some of the local clubs, the ones in town and a little bit out of town. He couldn't drink, but he could go in and shoot the bull with total strangers. A lot of bull. Justin was a master of bull-slinging, and sometimes he went too far and got other folks mad. He had opinions about everything, whether he knew anything about it or not, and he liked to show off and talk real big. I guess he figured that was a trait of being from Texas. He was always like that, even when we were young boys, and he was all the time getting into fights. Most times I didn't accompany him because I had homework.

But on the weekend a couple of times I went with him, and I saw him in action, just a-bragging or putting some other fellow down, and he got *this* close to getting into a big-time fight with some big-time boys. I warned him about it, but he shrugged me off, said it was all just for fun, and he could handle some drunks if he needed to.

But what really got on my nerves was when Justin stayed home. Then he would lounge around in nothing but his underwear, and it was awful hard for me to keep from staring at him. He was awesome, just this solid block of smooth tanned muscle! He would sit in the den watching TV, his legs spread, and sometimes, almost like he wasn't thinking about it, he'd reach down and dig into his crotch. I don't know if he did it on purpose or to get my attention, but it was awfully distracting. We lived in a small apartment with only one bedroom. Justin slept on the couch, all the time promising he'd get a rollaway bed. There'd be times I would stay up late doing homework at the little kitchen table, and I'd glance at him on the couch in the dark, sleeping in nothing but those BVDs, and I swear on a couple of occasions I'd see him playing with himself. His eyes looked to be closed, but there was no mistaking that motion! I'd eventually have to get up and go in the bedroom to study.

Other than those two things, it was good living with Justin. It was almost like we were a...I don't know...a *married* couple or something. All we needed was each other. Nobody else crowded in on the picture. We'd talk about girls and things, sure, but we never went out with any, and we didn't seem to feel the lack. We were okay as long as we had each other.

Well, one Friday night, Justin decided he wanted to go out. He asked me, but I turned him down again. I had a big chemistry exam that following Monday, and I had to get in all the studying before then I could. He looked at me like he couldn't believe I would turn down a chance to go barhopping because *I had to study.* He just thought that was the most pathetic thing and told me I was letting life pass me by. It pissed me off some, and I let him know. I told him I was studying to be something and didn't want to end up a no-count bum like him. Well, that pissed *him* off, and he left, cussing me under his breath. I didn't want to hurt his feelings or anything, but I was stressed out from studying and didn't feel like putting up with anybody's shit, you know?

I worked so hard that night I fell asleep at the kitchen table with all my books and papers underneath me and almost didn't hear the doorbell ringing. My head shot up. I looked at the clock on the kitchen wall. Through blurry eyes I saw that it was three thirty in the morning. The buzzer kept sounding. I got up, all groggy, to answer it. I opened the door, and there stood a police officer, a young guy in his suit and hat and with his gun belt on and everything.

"Yeah. Yes. What's the matter?" I managed to say to him.

"You live here?" he asked.

I started to say something smart-assed back but didn't think it was a good idea. "Yes."

"Do you share this apartment with a Justin Michael Thulon?"

I nodded.

"And your name?"

I told him.

"And what's your relationship to Mr. Thulon?"

I broke. Couldn't help it. It was so late, and I was still stranded, at least partway, in dreamland. "My roommate. My friggin' roommate. My best friend. Now could you tell me what the problem is, Officer?"

For some reason he didn't smart-ass back at me, and when I looked him in the eye, I could see there was more than a "matter." Something bad had happened. He had come to tell me something really bad about Justin. The panic knocked my irritation out of the way.

And he did. He said Justin had been at the Look-Out bar that evening and had gotten into some kind of argument with another man. They were going at each other with fists, although about what the police didn't yet know. The bar manager told them to get out. They did. But the fight resumed in the parking lot. They cussed each other and finally went to hitting. The other fellow pulled out a gun and shot twice. Both shots hit Justin in the abdomen. He survived the trip to the emergency room but died once they got him on the operating table.

I tell you, the next few hours were like a bad dream. I can't possibly explain in words how I felt. It was like some wild animal had got loose in my insides and was just gnawing away. That police officer told me I'd have to go down and identify the body, and I'd be the one to have to tell Justin's family and all that, and the only thing I could think of was, *We argued, me and Justin. He left here mad at me, and I didn't get to tell him I'm sorry!* Man, you would have to look in a baby carriage to find something that cried as much as I did. Oh, I did. Right in front of people. It didn't matter. That was my best friend on that cold slab in the morgue. That was my brother, and more, in that casket in that little church in Bolt, Texas. They had him all dressed up in a suit and tie, something I'd never seen Justin in, and his face shone so shiny and bright, I almost leaned down to kiss it.

When we got back to South Carolina after the funeral, my mama and daddy had to take me home with them. There was no way I could go back to that apartment, empty of Justin Thulon.

No, I went back home and lay on my bed and stared at the walls until, eventually, I went on off to sleep.

Well, some time passed, but the hurt from losing Justin was still pretty tender. He stayed on my mind all the time, 24/7. It seems everywhere I went I could see him, and these were in places he had probably never even been. It occurred to me in a sorrowful way that while Justin lived in South Carolina we had not really done the things we used to do growing up as boys in Texas— play sports, go four-wheeler riding, or fishing. And I thought, *I'll dust off my rod and reel and head to the water and catch a big one for ol' Justin.*

My granddaddy owned some land outside of town, with a pond. I didn't know if there were even any fish. But it didn't matter. It was just the idea of being outside in the warm, wonderful, sunshiny weather, the grass green as a frog's back, the breeze coming cool off the blue face of the pond. I lay back in the grass at some point and closed my eyes. Right away I saw Justin—the naked Justin, the way I had pictured him that night in my bedroom at home: naked and muscular and sporting a big ol' boner in front of him. It seemed obscene in a way thinking about him like that and him gone and all, but I couldn't help it. And pretty soon I saw myself with him, naked too, us coming together, embracing, and this time something more—kissing. Hungrily, our mouths just fierce for each other, our hands going crazy up and down each other's body. The image got me all tingly. My hands went down to the crotch of my pants. I was hard. I rubbed myself. I shouldn't have. It seemed, well, kind of sacrilegious. Then I had an even crazier idea. I stood up and took off my clothes. That's right! I got naked as a jaybird in the great outdoors, not a stitch on. If somebody came along, I'd say I was about to go skinny-dipping. But really I didn't care.

This was for Justin, I figured. I lay back down in the grass and brought up the image again of me and Justin going at it and played with myself, jerking myself really hard. It felt good but hurt too—the idea of something that never would be. I moaned and cried too, the tears rushing down my face while my right hand went crazy on my dick. I called Justin's name over and over while I watched in my mind how we loved each other with our hands and our mouths and our dicks. I got real close to coming, right on the very point, when I heard a voice over me: "Damn, Brandon, I never knew you were hung like that, boy!"

My eyes flew open. I let out a holler. The sun blinded me a minute till I shielded it with my hand. And there above me stood...it couldn't be him, but who the hell else could it have been? Justin Thulon! Right over me. Naked as I was. Dripping wet, the pond water flashing over his skin like diamonds and rubies. He smiled down at me and pointed at my dick. "Of course I never got a chance to see you when you were grown, now did I?"

"Justin!" I sat up.

"Who the hell else, man?" he answered with a laugh. I rubbed my eyes once, twice, three times, three times more, and never did I get rid of him. He was still there, naked and piled with golden-brown muscles and a hard-on that nearly touched my chin.

"But how?"

"Huh?"

"How did you get back here? You're gone."

"I reckon there was a little bit of unfinished business that had to be taken care of." And then he quit smiling and the humor left his voice and he went down to me right there on the ground, taking me back to the ground with him with one of his huge, smooth arms. He didn't say any more. He leaned over to kiss me. It felt real! It felt like a man's mouth and a man's moustache and goatee. It sure tickled like one. His tongue flicked out of his mouth and danced on my lips a minute before moving down to my hard and sweaty nipples. He sucked one and then the other, bit them, then let his tongue do its little dance on them again and went on. He circled my navel with his tongue, and pretty soon he reached my crotch, where my dick stood hard and heavy like some flagpole in the middle of things.

"So damn big," he repeated in a breathless voice and then licked it like he had everything else. He was thorough. He didn't let one inch of my dick escape the swipe of his tongue. Pretty soon he had the head in his mouth and he was pushing his face down the length of the whole shaft the best he could. He choked and came back up then went down again. This second time he held the thing longer and tickled the head with his tonsils. I just squirmed on the ground and dug one hand in the grass and the other into his beefy shoulder. He bounced up and down on me with his face, taking in as much as he could. His free hand wandered over my balls and farther down. He even played with my feet a minute. Then the hand crept back up and found its way between my legs.

"I always thought you had the cutest damn ass, Brandon," he told me, once he'd let my dick go. I spread my legs so he could explore me further. He had his middle finger between my asscheeks and was wiggling it into the crack. He had trouble getting into the hole right away, but pretty soon he was finger-pumping me and sucking my dick again at the same time. It was all too good to believe. It had to be a dream, but it felt so real! It felt selfish too, me getting all that pleasure. So I worked myself around on the ground so that I had hold of his thick dick and was sucking it too. It was the first time I had ever done it. I was sure I was no good at it, probably not putting the kind of pressure on him that made him feel good. But I tried. And he moaned and told me it was good. And he must have been right, because it wasn't long before he called out to me that he was about to shoot off, and sure enough, almost as soon as I had him out of my mouth, he was firing long strings of cum into the grass. His body tensed up then released. But he never stopped sucking me until I felt my own climax coming on. I told him so. He took me out of his mouth and jerked me real good. And then the most intense feeling went through me, coming up through my nuts into my belly to the tips of my nipples, and I fired my stuff into the air and onto Justin's hand. It was the best thing I had ever felt in my life.

He lay next to me afterward and caressed me while I got my breath back. Then, overcome, I fell onto him.

"I'm sorry, man," I told him as I sobbed into his shoulder, "about calling you a bum and all. I didn't get to tell you before you left. Then I never saw you again."

He laughed softly. "I don't even know what the hell you're talking about."

"It doesn't matter, I guess," I said. "It only matters that you're back. For good. Right?"

He shrugged. "For a little while anyway."

My eyes got wide. My voice went hoarse like it was changing for the first time. "You mean you're going to leave again?"

He kissed my wet cheek. "Don't worry about that. Just enjoy right now. Okay?" I nodded kind of halfheartedly. Then he lifted my chin and said, "You know what I'd like right now?" When I shook my head, he went on. "I'd like you to fuck the living meanness out of me!"

I laughed and shook my head. "What?" I had always thought, in my fantasies anyway, that if anal sex went on, it'd be Justin skewering me. Then I said, joking, "I ain't sure I got enough dick to do that!"

I lay on my back. Justin worked between my legs with his

mouth and hands to get me hard again. When I was hard enough, he squatted on me, lowering himself down on my dick. It went in easy, which made me wonder how many dicks had been up his butt, or if this easiness was on account of his being a spirit and all. It didn't matter. He rode me like I was a bronco and seemed to enjoy every minute of it. He had such a sweet smile on his face the whole time, with his eyes closed. He jacked himself hard and played with his right tit, squeezing and pinching the tip, till I took over the job for him. He looked so...well...*beautiful,* riding me like that and smiling. The sight of him put as much of a feeling in my heart as it did my dick.

"I love you," I told him as he bounced away. "I love you, Justin Thulon, and always will, no matter where the hell you are or *what* the hell you are. No matter." And the tears just streamed down my cheeks and blinded me for a little bit. But through the shimmer I could make out Justin nodding and smiling even wider. Then he grunted and whimpered, and my hand and belly were soaked with his white stuff. And at the same time the switch turned on in my balls and the tingly feeling was rising up in me. Justin knew it and clamped down hard on my dick to get the most of it. And I bucked on the ground and twisted and cried out until I had every last bit of that hot stuff out of my system.

Justin fell on me and embraced me and I hugged back, and it was the best feeling I ever had. I held him so tight, just damned and determined he wouldn't get away again. I wouldn't let him! He kissed my face and ruffled my hair and rubbed up gently against me so our bodies were stuck together with sweat and goo. The wind came gentle off the pond. The sun was warm gold on our bodies. There wasn't any way I wouldn't nod off to sleep with so much goodness and comfort around me. And that's what I did. I slept.

When I woke, my arms were empty. "Justin?" I called out right away and sat up. I looked around. He was nowhere. I stood, still naked, and walked around looking for him. Nothing. I went to the edge of the pond and stared into it, wondering if he had gone back there (if that had been the place he'd come from, that is). But there was only water and silt and a stray bass or two shooting through the coolness. My heart was heavy. I sat on the ground and put my head in my hands and started to cry again. It had all been a dream, the whole thing. A sweet dream that seemed so real. But now it was gone. I'd never *really* touched Justin or tasted him like I had always wanted to.

I fell back on the grass and looked up at the sky, and through my tears I saw something really peculiar. Hot almighty! And I'm not making this up, I swear. I'll swear it on a stack of Bibles and my own dear mama's grave that I saw what I'm saying I saw. In the sky, which was otherwise blue and clear as could be, there were words written in heavy white letters, like they had been made out of clouds, and they said this: TO BRANDON WITH LOVE, JUSTIN.

And I cried, and I cried. And, years later, I still do.

THE CURTAIN STORE

Anthony McDonald

It wasn't love at first sight. But it was attraction at first sight. And it was mutual, though I didn't know it then. We were both sixteen.

I'd landed a Christmas holiday job at our local theater, thanks to my grownup sister who worked there. I was going to operate one of the follow spots during the run of the panto-mime: *Aladdin* this year. I met the chief electrician a few days in advance, and he took me up the seemingly endless staircase to the back of the gallery. Two big spotlights were installed there, with a seat for each operator, on either side of the central aisle, behind the back row of seats. I say seats, but right up there in the gods they were actually benches. (Downstairs, the stalls and dress circle were all gilt and red plush.) I was shown how to swivel my light and move the barrel up and down. *Like an antiaircraft gun*, I thought. I was shown how to use the dimmer, following instructions received through headphones from the lighting box behind the stalls. My sister obligingly walked to and fro across the front of the stage, far below us and brilliantly lit, so that I had the chance to practice making the beam follow her, instead of waiting till I made an idiot of myself at the tech.

All casuals, as we were called, were summoned and met each other for the first time, in the green room an hour before the technical rehearsal started. Green room sounds grand, but it was nothing of the sort. It was a wide, windowless, linoleum-floored passageway between the dressing rooms and the stage. It was furnished with threadbare sofas from which the stuffing was escaping, a sink, a kettle and a fridge.

The stage manager divided the backstage crew into teams and handed them black clothes to wear. The assistant stage managers took charge of them and off they went. Which left the two of us.

I'd noticed Charlie at once, of course. Couldn't not. Our eyes met across a crowded green room... I know, but it really was like that. We were easily the youngest there. I guessed he was about sixteen, like me, and he, like me, was small for his age. Small but not scrawny. Now that the room was nearly empty I could see more of him. There was space for me to notice that his very tight jeans were roundly filled with muscular, trim thighs and calves, prominent buttocks and, at the front, a jaunty little dome that seemed to announce: look what I've got. I knew already that I was attracted to boys, not girls, and this worried me quite a lot. But all I'd ever done, and all I thought I'd ever do, was look.

"Know what you're doing and where to go?" the stage manager asked us. We said yes. He showed us where we could stow our coats and pullovers. No blacks for us: just the jeans and T-shirts we already had on. We pulled off our redundant pullovers. It was cold in the streets outside but at the top of the house it would be hot, especially behind those lamps. "I'm Tim," I said. "Charlie," my new acquaintance answered, and stuck out his hand. We climbed the stairs together. Not one in front and one behind but side by side.

There is a special kind of darkness in a theater when the houselights are down and the stage lights are up. It's dark yet not dark at the same time. Emergency lighting brands the word EXIT on your retina in underwater green. This is how the night must appear to cats.

There was enough light for me to see in my peripheral vision the side view of my fellow follow spot. During the next days I memorized every contour of that view, across the aisle, just out of reach. (We could have held hands across the aisle, I suppose, but obviously we did not.) I can bring it all to mind today: the springy, taut, bow curve of his thigh; his short, straight nose and biggish lips; the proud young muscles of his forearm and bicep. Little by little, then, I learned those details of beauty, as technical rehearsal was followed by full-dress, then day after day the people poured in by the hundreds, until even the gallery was full. I remember the noise, the kids, the heat.

Because we were the youngest two, we gravitated together in the green room during breaks. We went to different schools. Otherwise we'd have known each other already. But because we were both easygoing characters, inclined to like rather than compete with new people we met, we got along together very well. You could almost say we became friends. But all the time we stood or sat together, drinking oily tea and talking about school or last night's TV, I was imagining myself tearing off his tight jeans and... My imagination failed to come up with exactly what would happen next. I only knew that, whatever it was, I wanted it. I felt like King Lear, in the play I was then studying. *I will do such things, what they are, yet I know not, but they shall be the terrors of the earth.* Although Lear was talking about something else.

When you're sixteen you are very aware of who you fancy, but often quite slow on the uptake when it comes to noticing who fancies you. At least that was my case. So it didn't cross my mind that all my lustful thoughts about Charlie might be mirror images of Charlie's thoughts about myself.

Until that Saturday.

The stage manager asked the two of us if we'd like to earn a little extra cash. One of the rooms beneath the stage, the curtain store, was in a mess, he told us. A fire hazard. If there was an inspection the fire chiefs would have a fit. It was arranged that Charlie and I would go in the following Saturday morning and tidy it up.

There were a number of interconnecting rooms in the bowels of the theater below the stage. The band had to make its way through them on the way to the orchestra pit. One room contained small items of furniture, another, which we explored at the start of our visit that morning, was full of an intriguing assortment of props. We saw some broadswords and gingerly took them into our hands for a few seconds, feeling their balance and weight. The last room, the curtain store, answered to the stage manager's description of it: a mess. Tabs and drapes of all sizes, colors and thicknesses, from plush red velvet numbers to plain black masking had been thrown down by people in a hurry, month after month, instead of being folded and stacked on shelves. Most of the floor was occupied by a sort of compost heap of curtain, about four feet deep.

Two people folding theater curtains go about it much like two people folding tablecloths or sheets; it just takes longer, and requires a lot more muscular effort, which becomes more noticeable with the passing of time. Again and again Charlie and I walked toward each other with a fold of fabric scooped up from the floor, passed it into the clasp of the other's outstretched hands, and backed away to pick up the next section of curtain and create a new fold. It was like performing some absurd variation on an ancient courtly dance. Every time we came together, hands touching hands, we felt the warmth of each other's breath, looked searchingly into each other's eyes. And whatever that thing was that I wanted to do with Charlie, I wanted it more with every series of forward steps, with every pleat. I felt that something in me was being wound up to a dangerously high pitch, like a violin string, and that if this went on much longer, like a violin string it would snap. Maybe the whole instrument would smash too.

But Charlie snapped first. He suddenly dropped the heavy velvet tab we were working on, grabbed a smaller one and shot out through the door with it. I gazed after him, rooted where I was and perplexed. But in a second he was back. The curtain was draped around him dashingly, like a Roman cape, and he carried two of the broadswords we'd handled earlier in the other room. He held one out to me.

Obviously I needed my own curtain cape. I plucked one up at random and luckily it was not impossibly big. I threw it around me with an optimistic swish, hoping it might achieve the same swashbuckling appearance as Charlie's did, and then we began to fence.

Actually, to say we fenced would be seriously to over-describe what now took place. A broadsword is a mighty heavy thing and neither of us was very big. Also, I didn't know how to fence. Neither did he. So all we did was stand and face each other, rather slowly clashing the sides of our weapons together, forming iron crosses each time in the air between us. I think we were both aware that had we tried anything bolder or more dramatic we would probably have taken off each other's head. Even so, the noise was pretty good.

Then Charlie dropped his sword and ran (ran three feet? More like jumped) toward me, forcing me to drop my weapon too. Excitedly Charlie threw his cloak around my shoulders so that it enveloped us both, and his body pressed against mine. *Oh, god, I thought, he'll discover that I'm hard, and how embarrassing that's going to be.* But I didn't spend long thinking that.

Charlie had got one hand inside the cloak and was fumbling with something. I wasn't quite ready to believe it was his zip. But then I felt him tug mine down and had to believe it. Our two cocks seemed to emerge of their own accord, both hard, both hot, mine pressed up against his, unseen in the curtained dark.

We abandoned our hiding place, letting our cloaks fall to the floor. And discovered that the sight of our two cocks was not enough. We wanted balls too, and pubes, and tops of thighs. It was less than a second before our jeans were halfway down our legs.

The sight of Charlie's partial nakedness, all that part of him between pulled-up T-shirt and pulled-down pants was the most wonderful thing ever. It etched itself upon my inner eye and is with me to this day. His cock, short, thick and circumcised, stood straight up against his belly, flattening his scanty pubes. You couldn't have got a cigarette paper behind it. Mind you, the same went for mine.

We threw each other, toppling, onto the still deep pile of curtains on the floor. Each took the other's cock in hand and pumped it at ferocious speed. We lasted less than thirty seconds, I think. Then our milk came gushing out of us. We let it find its way down through the curtain pile.

We found it impossible to chat normally and look each other in the eye during our green room breaks that Saturday matinee and evening. The shock and dislocation of self that occurred as a result of my first sexual experience with another were even greater than they'd been on the occasion of my first private orgasm, in bed, two years before. I felt that Charlie and I had somehow broken something—like breaking a family heirloom, or something of that kind. During the Sunday that followed I was glad not to have him around. I didn't want to face the confusion that had been caused between the two of us. Caused by him. Caused by me.

But guess what? By Monday evening my cock was ready for Charlie again, even if my bruised soul was not. When we met in the green room at seven o'clock we exchanged a shy grin, which somehow accepted and explained that, though we weren't yet quite ready to speak, given time we would be.

We did speak. Later that evening. And a few days later we found a moment, and an excuse, to visit the curtain store together once again. It wasn't easy to arrange such a tryst without being noticed. We only managed it six more times before the panto ended its run. And then we parted. We said we'd phone each other, but we never did. Life moves on quickly when you're sixteen. We went to different schools, had different friends. Things happened to us. We did other things. We grew up.

The theater bug had bitten hard and deep. When I was at university I got involved with the theater in the town, working backstage part time, on and off. Around the time I graduated a vacancy for an ASM arose there. I applied and—no big surprise—got the job. Degree in economics? Forget that.

Over the next few years I moved up the ladder fast. If you were willing to up sticks and move to another part of England or Scotland hundreds of miles away—something that many people were not prepared to do—you could do that. ASM means assistant stage manager. Most theaters employ three or four. DSM means deputy stage manager, and there is only one.

I was DSM in Glasgow at the age of twenty-two, stage manager at Plymouth at twenty-three, then production manager—a senior post with big budgets to control and ten full-time staff to manage—at twenty-four. Aged twenty-five I was the general manager—top dog except for the director of productions—at a theater in Wales.

You learn fast in that job. You discover that the manager is, in the last resort, the changer of roller towels, fixer of decrepit ball-cock valves in the toilets and un-blocker of drains. He must stand up to the bullying of directors on the board and hold his own against experienced senior staff, some of whom have been in post since before he was born. I found myself the licensee of two bars, one in the circle, one in the stalls, and would have to attend court every year or two, dressed in a suit, to plead my case for those licences to be renewed. I was also, de facto, a member of the Regional Theaters Council, which meant attending a meeting in London once a year, again in a suit. The same suit. The only suit.

There was a certain grim delight, I found, in meeting on an equal footing those venerable souls who had interviewed me for jobs during the past four years. Especially those who'd happened to turn me down. At the first meeting of the council that I attended I was by far the youngest present. I already knew, or thought I knew, that I was the youngest general manager of any regional theater in the UK. But then I saw him, also in a suit, across the... (Yes, yes, I know.) Across the crowded room. I remembered at once not only who he was, but that he was two months younger than me. But never was a record holder more delighted to relinquish his title.

There was barely time to say hallo before the business of the meeting began. At least, with that hallo I'd established that he remembered me. We sat together. From the corner of my eye I could see the taut bow curve of his thigh in the close-fitting trousers of his suit. That familiar short, straight nose. The full lips of his handsome mouth. His head of shining black curls. He'd grown a little taller in the years since I'd known him, and so had I, but in both our cases not very much.

But if someone fancied you at the age of sixteen there is no guarantee that nine years on they still will. So much happens in those particular years, so much of your life is crammed into them. You've changed. You've learned to earn a crust for a start, and you've taken some knocks in the process. You've been in love a couple of times and had your young heart broken once or twice.

And, quite importantly, I had to remind myself that not every teenager who's played with another boy's cock grows up to be gay. If that were the case we wouldn't be worried about over-populating the planet. Rather the reverse.

It was an afternoon meeting. Neither of us actually rose to speak during the course of it. It was a first time for both of us, and the cockiness with which we'd arrived and greeted our older peers had quickly evaporated. We were overawed by the seniority and expert knowledge of the other delegates, intimidated by the very thing that made us special there: our shared, exceptional, youth.

When the meeting was closed and people stood and general chatter broke out, Charlie turned to me and said, with a diffidence in his voice I hadn't heard before, "Do you have time to go for a drink?"

I smiled, reassuringly I hoped (though it's a clever man who knows his own smiles), and said, "Yes." Did I have time? *The rest of my life.*

The meeting had been at Covent Garden. We walked to Rose Street and into the old Lamb and Flag. We bought pints of

Young's bitter and sat among the age-black furniture and beams. We talked about how we'd got to the positions in the theater that we now held. There were two standard routes to the job of general manager. I'd come up by one of them, Charlie by the other. His way had lain on the other side of the safety curtain: front of house. Box office assistant, box office manager, front of house manager, PR and advertising manager, and now here he was, doing the same job that I did, but in Cambridge, two hundred miles away from me. Like me he'd achieved his rapid rise by going for jobs again and again, in no matter what godforsaken part of the country they might be. Like me his track had crisscrossed the kingdom. It was surprising that it hadn't, until now, crossed mine.

We had so much to talk about. We could have talked for hours. Actually we did. On our third pint I looked at my watch for the first time and saw it was nearly eight. Then Charlie said, "I suppose you're married and all."

I didn't reply at once. I'd wanted, yet not wanted, to ask the same question. His answer of yes would have sent the evening on a downward curve. Not at once, but gently. We would have parted friends in an hour's time and promised to stay in touch. Only we wouldn't have done. We might meet again at the next annual meeting of the Regional Theaters Council. If we still had our jobs then. Charlie was looking at me. There was something a bit despondent in his eyes. Time to answer. I said, "No. What about you?"

"No. Nor me," he said, and looked away.

Charlie, the bolder of the two of us, had done his best. Now I had to help. "Actually," I said, "I'm not very likely to be. I've turned out gay."

He said very softly, "Me too." I didn't try to meet his eye. I don't think he tried to meet mine.

There were stages to this, I realized. The conversation would proceed tantalizingly, as if we were unwrapping a gift parcel that might, but only might, have something inside, or disassembling a Russian doll, or unlocking some door or treasure chest with an elaborate succession of catches and bolts. There was only one order in which to proceed; the sequence could not be shortcut. And when the process was complete, the treasure chest might yet prove empty, and there be nothing behind the door.

"Boyfriend back in Wales?" he tentatively asked.

I shook my head. "No time." I'd actually had no sex with anyone since starting my newest job, pressure of work and time being elements of this situation, though not the only ones, but I wasn't going to volunteer all this just yet.

"Ditto, ditto," he said. Then he looked at me. His blue eyes looked troubled now. Surprising myself, I laughed. Not rudely, not loudly, but I laughed. And he reacted by doing the same. His eyes looked less troubled now. Curious perhaps. "Do you remember the curtain store?" he asked.

I was surprised into a sort of splutter. "How could I ever forget?"

There was another pause, while we looked at each other. We still didn't have absolute proof that we fancied each other. Hindsight is one thing, dealing with the situation on the spot is quite another. Charlie spoke. "I suppose you have to get back to Wales tonight."

"Work in the morning," I said. "Same as you." I could sense, rather than see, Charlie's disappointment. I wriggled. "I mean, I should go back." I paused for a split second. "We could catch a show, I suppose."

"Yeah," said Charlie. "But isn't that a bit too much like work? I mean, for you and me. Doing the jobs we do. Show every night." He gave me a look. The kind of look that writers call quizzical. "We could go for a meal. You can talk in a restaurant, you can't at a show." There was a slight pause during which he looked away. "We could get a room for the night." He waited apprehensively for my reply.

That switch from bold to diffident went to my heart. But that wasn't the only thing. The idea of spending a night together set off such a rush of feelings that it was like a firework display inside me. "Let's do that," I said quietly.

When you work for a boss you have to phone them and make your excuse if you're going to arrive late. When you are the boss you have to phone a member of your staff and do the same thing. Charlie and I got our phones out there and then and phoned our front of house managers—the most senior people present at our two theaters at that time of evening. When you tell them you're going to be detained in London and won't be at work till tomorrow lunchtime they know exactly what this means. Charlie and I mugged grimaces at each other as we trotted out our lame half-truths.

We didn't have to go far in Covent Garden to find a good restaurant—an Italian one. Then we found the nearest cheap hotel. "Twin room?" the woman receptionist asked.

"Can you make it a double?" Charlie asked. Two months younger than me, but twice as brave. As he'd been in the curtain store all that time ago. The receptionist did blink, but then she politely handed him a key.

We looked solemnly into each other's blue eyes as we undid each other's shirt and took it off. For practical reasons we then dealt with our own shoes and socks. But we returned to each other in order ceremoniously to remove the trousers of each other's suit, pull down each other's underwear, release each other's springing cock. Then we stood back to admire our work.

I thought he looked gorgeous. Not big, but gently muscled, still boyish. A little tongue of dark hair licked up from below, straight up the center line of his belly where it petered out. There was no hair on his chest; as if to compensate, his nipples were proudly big. Back in the curtain store days we'd only ever seen the middle third of this view of each other that we now appraised in full. We'd known the other's body only from belly button to knees. I already knew I'd love his legs when they were revealed. But, heavens, I even found his knees beautiful. Even his long-toed feet. I told him so.

"You're beautiful all over," he said, very solemnly and running a finger tremulously down my chest. "We're not much bigger that we were," he went on thoughtfully, as his finger encountered the resistance of my own little flame of belly hair, flaring upward from my pubes. Then he grinned. "Except in the matter of this." He gently touched the up-reaching tip of my penis, which immediately caused the foreskin to slide back and a dewdrop to appear like magic on its tiny lips. "How we've both grown."

It was no longer true that a cigarette paper could not have been slid between our bellies and stiff cocks. Now a cigarette packet would have done. But that's the price you pay for growing bigger, growing heavier. Growing up. With my own forefinger I touched the chunky head of his cut, sturdy cock. It reacted just like mine had done. Spilt a little juice. We giggled. Then, serious again, we moved into each other till we touched at every possible point. We began to kiss.

It wasn't long before we had to move to the bed. My cock was threatening to spill over, weighty with a load that seemed to be already gathering inside. I guessed it was the same for him. Neither of us had brought condoms: it was a business meeting we'd come to London for, or so we'd thought. And we didn't want, tonight at any rate, to have to interrogate each other with uncomfortable questions, possibly to hear answers we didn't want. I was certain of my own status—negative, but Charlie didn't know that, just as I didn't know his. We lay clasped together, duvet pulled down so we could see each other properly, and did exactly what we'd done on the curtain pile all those years before. Because of that bank of experience from way back we were supremely comfortable and confident with each other's physicality and need. We pulled just far enough apart at the end to have the satisfaction of seeing each other's creamy spurt, just as we'd done when we were little more than kids, then lay pressed together as if we might stay that way for all time.

"I think about you very often," Charlie said, close to my ear.

"Me too," I said. It was true. The memory of Charlie was a kind of background rumble through all my waking moments and had been for all those years.

"Even when you're doing *that?*" he asked, and I felt his hand clasp and squeeze my melting dick, to leave me in no doubt about what *that* meant.

I admitted it. "Occasionally," I said.

"Me too," he said, and chuckled, and fell asleep.

We did *that* again in the small hours, and again just before we got up. But in between those landmark points in time we both half woke when a blade of steel-gray light was prising open the new day. I murmured to Charlie, "I don't want dawn to come." He said, "I never want to leave this bed." We were wallowing in the warmth of each other. Warm tummies, thighs, chests, shoulders and encircling arms. Warm pricks. Newly vulnerable in our shared warm, intermittently wet, nakedness. He said, "Don't want to go back to Cambridge." I said, "Don't want to go to Wales." But all those things had to happen, and they did.

* * *

My phone burned like an ember in my pocket all that day. Which of us would make contact first? How long before we did? What were we ever going to say? Or text?

It was Charlie, at nearly ten o'clock that night, who made the call. Bold, tender Charlie, not for the first time, cracked first. It wasn't a text. He gave me his voice. "I want to see you, Tim," he said.

"Me too," I answered. No other answer was remotely possible. We had unlocked the doors to each other, unlocked the treasure chests, taken apart those Russian dolls, but only so far as to deliver a one-night stand, even if that had been a very lovely one. But there was farther to go, more work to be done, more locks to pick.

The following morning I woke up and saw Charlie's face immediately, as if it were really before my eyes. I knew already what that meant. I knew I'd see it morning after morning until we met again. As I made my solitary breakfast I imagined him making his and wondered, pathetically, if he was thinking of me. He phoned an hour later. "I saw you in my mind when I woke up," he said. "Sorry," he went on. "Do I sound sad? But I just can't stop thinking about you." I told him that was just fine and that it was the same with me.

We met in London that weekend. We could have seen a show, gone to a club. Neither of those options appealed to us in the least. We sat talking in a pub, pouring out our lives and thoughts like mountain streams in spate. We drank each other's words, each other's intimate revelations, with the sensual joy of parched travelers.

Mutual lust can be great. Charlie and I had acknowledged that during our overnight stay in London a few days ago. But it has a sell-by date, like a cut flower. Only sometimes does it put out roots, become a living plant and start to grow into something bigger than it was when it began. Talking to Charlie, getting to know him better that evening, I dared to believe, just to begin to believe, that something bigger might grow in us.

We ate at a Thai restaurant. We checked into the same cheap hotel. Deadpan, the receptionist gave us the key to the same room. We'd both brought condoms, and we laughed at that. We made love. I was able to think that expression this time: we made love. The previous week I hadn't dared to think it.

A week later we met in Cambridge. I went to the flat Charlie shared with a young architect, who was straight, but easy around gay men. The following weekend Charlie came to Wales. I too shared a flat, with two young teachers, one of each sex. They too were straight but had no problem with the idea of *us*—as Charlie and I (though still only privately, separately) now identified ourselves. I showed Charlie round my theater in the dark quiet of Sunday morning. We had a curtain store in the backstage area. We looked at each other and had to smile. Then—tacky was it? Can't be helped—we went in there and did *that*, for old times' sake. (Though we were more careful not to stain the curtains. We were responsible managers now and these particular curtains were a responsibility of mine. I didn't want some ASM unfolding them and saying, "Dear god, who did that?") Later I walked with Charlie to the station. This time I was the bold one. "Are we falling in love, Charlie?" I asked.

"You may be," he answered, poker-faced. Then he grinned. "Me, I've already fallen. Pretty bloody hard. Pretty damn deep." There comes a moment sometimes when two people who thought they'd been in love a couple of times before in the course of their lives realize they haven't. For Charlie and me that moment had been reached.

* * *

The long-distance phase of our relationship lasted over a year. The transport costs were dismaying, and at times during the winter the rail network fell apart due to heavy snow, and one or other of us would be stranded for half a weekend at some remote and unheated railway junction. (In Britain the rail companies excuse themselves in this situation by explaining that the wrong type of snow has fallen.) We each spent our twenty-four-hour Christmas—the maximum that theater life allows—with our respective families, who lived only two miles apart, but there was no time for the upheaval and explanations that would have been involved in meeting up. Though we made up for that with a private feast of our own in Cambridge a few days later. Meeting me off a train on one of those snowy weekends, Charlie complained, "It's like bloody *Brokeback Mountain.* Talk about high-altitude fucks four times a year." On top of our long working weeks those weekends of tedious travel would have left most people exhausted, but it wasn't like that for two young men in love.

Then the front of house manager at Charlie's theater gave her notice in. She too was moving up the chain, going on to a bigger job somewhere else. Now it was my turn to be the bold one: I told Charlie I planned to apply for the vacancy created by her going. "You can't," he said. "It'd wreck your CV, spell the end of your career." He meant to sound shocked, but I heard other things in his voice: a kind of thrill; something like awe. I said, "So what?"

"No, but really…"

"Too late," I said. "My wrecked CV is already in the post. It'll land on your desk tomorrow morning."

I got the job, of course: the interviewing panel consisted simply of Charlie and his director of productions, an older gay man. It meant a big pay cut, and a lot of explaining to my parents, but there you go. I thought there'd be a lot of explaining to do at the theater in Wales, which I was leaving after little more than a year, but I was wrong. Apologetically I explained the situation to my PA. "Of course," she said, and took my hand. "We all knew. You silly goose. Best thing that could happen." I tried to give her a peck on the cheek by way of thanks but she wasn't expecting it and I ended up kissing her nose.

I moved to Cambridge and Charlie and I lived and worked together, day in day out, for a year that passed as quickly as a holiday. Then Charlie took a proposal to his board: for the post of front of house manager to be abolished, for as long as Charlie and I both worked at Cambridge. We'd combine our two jobs and share them, splitting the salaries equally. This was coming out at work in a very big way: it not only startled the board, it got a column or two, and a picture of the pair of us, in the local rag. But the proposal was passed, and now we take it in turn to wear the evening bow tie, take it in turn to face the assault course of the morning. It is an assault course, as all jobs are. We handle it okay. Better than okay, in fact. Being together gives us a strength we couldn't manage on our own. It's the strength that only one thing can give you: the strength that comes from love.

Cambridge is unique among British theaters, at least, among the ones I know, in that it provides a small apartment within the main building, for the front of house manager's use. That apartment is now ours. On Sundays, in the quiet time, it's almost as if the whole building is our home. A great eccentric mansion, furnished with several hundred chairs, a dozen mirrors in ormolu and gilt, and as many swords and costumes as anyone could wish for. Actually, we don't. We haven't turned into batty theater queens, and we don't hang around the building when we're free. We get out and go places, do things, just like anybody else.

On the other hand—I write this with a certain amount of embarrassment, and can already imagine smiles—there is a sizeable, often untidy, curtain store behind the stage. And just occasionally, very occasionally, for old times' sake, for the sake of memories which are silly and sentimental but also nice... I think I'll leave it there.

THE PRISONER

C. C. Williams

I surveyed the items arrayed on the stark, utilitarian bedspread of the guest room: khaki T-shirt; camouflage fatigues; a sandy, dun-colored officer's cap. Tucked neatly beneath the bed stood black combat boots so highly polished it was as if they were carved from obsidian. *I guess we're doing some paramilitary scene.*

Charley waited for me in his bedroom; he'd approached me earlier that night.

I had stopped by Tony's Bar & Grill after a late night at work and sat nursing a Tanqueray while a bored go-go boy gyrated to Lady Gaga's "Born This Way." At first I hadn't recognized Charley; he'd changed so much from our days at the academy. Gone was the vulnerable boy's face, shadowed with inexperience and bright with expectation. His face had filled out; ten years of life lay like a mask across his features. But the voice, soft and insistent, had remained the same. I had a hard time listening to him. While he spoke of joining the Marines and doing several tours of Iraq and Afghanistan, I shut my eyes. And there I saw his young eighteen-year-old face as it had been when we had lain together in the dark—intelligent and beautiful but innocent of the evil that men do.

Stripping off my jeans and polo, I began to don the military gear. Pulling the fatigues up over my thighs, I was surprised to find that we now wore the same size pants. In college I had always out-massed Charley, but our bodies had fit just right; his wiry sprinter's form merged with my wrestler's build, like muscle and sinew entwined on bone. The shirt stretched tight across my more muscular chest and biceps; a tear on the right shoulder opened wider as I pulled on the shirt. Lacing up the combat boots, I noticed a few milky stains around the toes. The spots marred the glossy blackness, and I thought of wiping them off. But I considered they might actually be part of the scene that awaited me. I put on the starched, sweet-smelling officer's cap and tucked some stray hairs behind my ears. I recalled the last time we had been together—a beautiful night, an awful night...

I had returned to our dorm room, worn out after wrestling practice, wanting just a shower and some mindless TV. I switched on the lights, tossing my gym bag on the floor.

"Leave 'em off." Charley's voice was thick and emotional, clogged with something raw. "Please."

Clicking off the fluorescent fixture, I looked to his bed where he lay on his belly, naked. The parted curtains let a splash of moonlight fall across him. He looked like an artsy postcard—except for the welts and livid bruises on his lower back, arms and legs.

"Oh, my god!" I rushed forward and knelt at his bedside. "Are you all right? What happened?"

"Nothing. I don't want to talk about it."

"Can I get you something? Water? Aspirin?" I blurted out, panicked, concerned. "We should go to the infirmary—"

"Shut up, just…" Charley sighed and broke down.

I fought a creeping sense of distance, a feeling of abandonment that pressed on my heart. "Should I leave you alone?"

He reached out, grabbing my hand. "No! Please don't." He squeezed my hand hard.

"What do you want me to do?" I climbed up and sat on the edge of his bed.

After a painful silence, he whispered, "Show me you care."

Just like so many times over the last eight months, I laid my hands on him, marveling at his satiny skin, pressing my fingers into the lithe muscles of his shoulders. I rubbed his back, and he moaned softly. My long fingers crept up his neck to tangle in his dirty-blond hair—it was longer than regulation and needed a trim. I massaged his scalp. Lowering my lips to the small of his back, I kissed around the red, inflamed skin, a crawling sense of dread nibbling at my mind. Dark thoughts invaded me, gray worries of the unknown scudded across my mind like clouds before the moon. Usually, I was breathless with wonder as I reveled in the sensations of his body, awash in a mixture of fear and joy, that stomach-fluttering feeling when you stand on the diving board, before surrendering to the cool breeze and the water that swallows you up.

My hands came to join my lips at his waist. Before I massaged his gorgeous butt, he winced. "Not there—not…tonight."

Sitting upright, I wiped his forehead. "Tell me what happened." I kissed his cheek, nuzzling at him, loving the softness of his day's growth of beard.

"Not yet," he breathed. "Love me everywhere, but not there tonight. Just love me, Jake."

Still dreading the silent unknown, yet moved by the aching

need in his voice, I took him in my arms and picked him up from the bed. Cradled like a baby, he clung to my neck and shoulders, embracing me as tightly as he could. We kissed, our mouths open, panting into each other. We drank from the saliva we exchanged; our tongues dueled for supremacy.

Breaking from the kiss, I licked at him, running my tongue over his lips, his chin, tasting the salt on his tear-stained cheeks. With pursed lips I pecked his cheekbones and eyebrows, blew cool air on his closed eyelids. I covered his nose with kisses, lapping at the bridge, his nostrils, again tasting the saltiness of his pain.

My passion increased as I worshipped him, fired by the feel of soft skin covering solid muscle. Entranced, I bit his neck, licked his shoulders and swallowed up each of his nipples. Straining my back and biceps, I covered his chest and belly with wet, hungry kisses; then lowered my mouth to his erect cock.

"Oh, *yeah!*" Charley gripped my hair. "Eat me up, man, eat me alive."

I sucked at his swollen cock head, swirling the tip of my tongue around the slit and nipping at the curve, clean cut around the edges. He bucked his eight-inch cock against my face, begging with his body to fuck my mouth. I'd become a pretty good cocksucker in the last eight months. Having had only fantasies, I had been inexperienced, but my slightly more experienced roommate had proven to be an excellent teacher.

"Put me down, Jake. I don't want you to hurt yourself." I obeyed, lowering him to the floor. Charley leaned against our dresser, spreading his thighs with a wince. His pale cock stood tall, curving out from his sandy bush. Grabbing his sinewy legs, I dove for his crotch, taking him in with every gulp of air I inhaled. Charley withdrew to some place in his head, arms behind his back, legs spread. Once he stroked my cheek. Once he grabbed his briefs and wiped my nose before snot ran down and mixed with my spit and his precome.

Jerking his rod, I gnawed on his hips and thighs; my nose pressed into his crotch. He smelled like woodsy air, boy sweat, and sex. Testosterone fired my brain, burning away my worries with bright desire. I still wore my wrestling singlet, and my stiff cock strained for release from my jockstrap. Like a dog I rubbed my dick against his calf.

"Yeah! Hump my fucking leg, boy. Hump away while I fuck your hand with my cock. Don't stop, asshole. Don't you dare stop."

Charley was unusually aggressive in his love talk, so I wondered what was playing out in his head. *Who are you talking to?*

"God, I want so much for you to fuck me right now. To bend me over and spread my white ass. Hock a big gob of snot down on my crack, and poke it in me with your thumb—running that thumb around my hole, opening it up for your big, veiny cock. You thrusting in and fucking me harder and harder. I'll pretend, yeah, pretend that you're going to fill me up for the rest of my life."

Unsure of what I was hearing, I looked up. "Do you want me to?"

His body writhed, and he grimaced in the moonlight. That meant he was getting close. "No! Just keep loving me hard like you're doing now. Aww, shit—"

Shuddering, he collapsed against me. His dick erupted, shooting a ropy load up onto my neck and shoulders. He continued to orgasm, letting go a second and third time, thickly coating my hand with his white cream. Never had I seen him shoot more than twice. Before I could grab for a towel, Charley was licking me clean. He seemed to have returned to the moment; he sighed. "I'm sorry. I was selfish. Let me suck you off."

"No," I replied. Standing, I pulled him up and hugged him. "I just wanted to make you feel good,"

"You sure did that!" He licked my jaw. "You'll never know how much."

Pushing away from him, I held him at arms' length. "Charley, tell me what happened—now!"

"I need a drink first." A moment later, dressed in his tattered bathrobe, he sipped whiskey from a Dixie cup. Contraband whiskey I kept far back under my bed. His fingers tapped on the cup as he paced the room. I stood by the dresser, confused, feeling embarrassed, still smelling of sex and wrestling practice. He took a deep breath. "You know Trey Hauser."

"The dumb-ass bully? Of course!" Hauser, a rich, legacy senior, regularly sought out and bullied the scholarship guys. He and his little gang were two years ahead of us.

"He's been harassing me for a while now—most of the year."

"Shit." I sat on my bed and poured myself more whiskey.

"He's been leaving notes in my books, my gym locker, even under the door. Notes that say things like *Cocksucker* or *Ass Licker*. He's cornered me after lunch, between classes, grabbing at my uniform and messing it up. He'll say, 'You're mine, fag,' or 'One of these days, I'll get you.'

"A couple of weeks ago he and three of his friends came at me. He called me a pussy and grabbed my nipple. They just laughed and watched me squirm. Then Trey said, 'Come on. Tell me what a pussy you are and I'll let go.' He squeezed so hard I had to obey or he'd have torn a hole in my fucking chest!"

That explained the ugly bruise; Charley's story about stabbing himself with a marking pen had been pretty lame.

"Well, a few days ago, I'd had enough. I told Trey I was going to report him to the Commandant. I don't know how much good it would do—Trey's father graduated with him, so they're like best buddies. But I threatened to tell him everything.

"'You'll be dead,' Trey said.

"'Fuck you,' I said. In fact, I was going to tell the Major tonight. But when you went to practice, Trey and his buddies showed up." Charley held out the paper cup, and I splashed in more liquor.

"The four of them grabbed me outside the front door, dragged me down to the boiler room and stripped me." Charley's hand shook as he sipped at the liquid. "Trey had brought along his razor strop—that pretentious fuck with his old-fashioned shaving kit! His friends held me down. I struggled and struggled; I just couldn't get away.

"He said, 'Bend him over.' They held my arms and legs, while Trey beat my ass with his strop. He said he wouldn't stop until I begged him to fuck me. I wouldn't." Charley shook his head, reliving the memory.

"I didn't even cry at first. He just kept hitting me and hitting me—god, it must've gone on for ten, fifteen minutes. Maybe longer! I could hardly breathe; it was like my ass was on fire. I finally broke down—I let out a scream and cried and cried. Trey and his buddies just laughed. I couldn't stand it anymore. I...begged...for it. And Trey...Trey gave it to me." He dashed tears away with the back of his wrist. Sniffling, he took a shot of whiskey.

Bile rose in my throat, burning away the mellowness of the whiskey. My heart ached with rage. My arms tensed; I wanted to pound something, pound on something again and again until there was nothing left.

"I..." I had no words.

Charley didn't move, just stood sipping from the crumpled paper cup. "It wasn't like us, Jake. It was...ugly, violent. Then...they...did it...too... I closed my eyes and imagined that

I was somewhere else, making love with you."

My anger gave way to sorrow. I remembered the first time we'd made love: how Charley had guided me to fuck him, nice and slow, tempering my pent-up desire into slower-burning passion. How each day I would anticipate the wavelike rhythms of our lovemaking at night, the way we would breathe into each other's mouths.

"I feel so ashamed." He choked back a sob.

"You have to report this." I touched his shoulder. "I'll stand with you, be your witness."

"What good would it do? Trey spotted me as a butt licker the minute I walked into this place." Charley shrugged off my hand and moved to face the window. Silvery light highlighted the tracks of tears on his face. I wanted to dry them, make the whole episode go away.

"It was just a matter of time before it came out." He leaned on the windowsill, swirling the cup, and then downed the rest of the liquor. "You know, people feel sorry for you, having to room with the likes of me."

"I said that I'll stand with you—I'll admit everything about me too."

"Why should you? Nobody suspects you're a fag. You're a wrestler. You're a man." He hurled *man* as if it were an obscenity. "I'm just the nelly little runner. Fuck. No matter how fast I run, they always catch me." He sat on his bed, cradling his head in his hands.

I wanted to show him that this time was different, to prove to him that not everyone was against him. But I didn't know how; in my heart I feared I was wrong, feared that my love wouldn't be enough. Apprehension throttled me and I had nothing supportive to say, so I sat on the floor, resting my head against his thigh, and stroked his calf. "Then we'll leave. We'll transfer out of here and go to a better school. I'll protect you. I'll never—ever—let anyone hurt you again."

Charley's hand stroked my hair. We held each other for a long time, cuddling together in the dark. He said only two words the rest of the night: "Thank you."

The next morning I awoke to find Charley gone.

In the following days nobody would tell me where he went. His parents hung up when I called; my letters were returned unopened. Confusion and heartache turned to bitterness as I finished out the year and then transferred to State, giving my folks a cock-and-bull story about the "lousy politics that prevented me from fulfilling my athletic potential."

Feeling sullen and rejected, I had sex with no one until three years later, when I took a lover in grad school. By then my broken heart had scabbed over and Charley entered my thoughts only rarely, usually when I buried myself in my lover's ass, rocking against his smooth back and listening to him purr with contentment.

Before leaving the guest room, I shook my head, clearing away the memories. I'd been so transported that now more than ever I regretted not standing up for Charley. *I should have gone after that fuckhead Trey, taken his strop and beat him senseless in front of his shitty friends.* I wondered what Charley thought. He'd not said a word about that night.

Entering Charley's room, I found myself transported into a different scene. The bedroom was austere: a gray-sheeted double bed against the wall, no rug, the only other furnishing standing opposite the bed—a wooden construction composed of a sturdy upright and a crossbeam; it resembled a crucifix. Desolation filled the room; the air itself felt devoid of any happiness, and that depressed me.

Leaning against the cross, Charley held his hands behind his back. Barefoot, he wore torn camouflage pants and a stained green tank top that clung to his well-developed torso. Dog tags hung from his neck, resting in the valley between his pecs. His hair was mussed, and he had smudged soot or something across his nose and cheeks. He stared at me, his eyes daring me to pass judgment on him. Again I was struck by how he had changed. Not just older, he'd become different: he was not the adult that my Charley would have become. His arc had been altered.

"I'm your prisoner of war." His voice sounded flat, matter-of-fact. His eyes never left mine. "You're responsible for inter-rogating me. I may have information vital to your cause. You've had me locked up for a week, starving me, but I haven't said shit so far. That's why you've brought me here. I need addi-tional...persuasion."

He flashed me a reassuring grin and the young Charley shone through for a moment. "Don't worry, Jake. I'll guide you through this."

Just as quickly the grin vanished, replaced with a sneer. "See those cuffs above my head? Put my hands in them, turn the key and place the key in your pocket."

Part of me wanted to say, "Let's cut the theater, get naked on the bed and fuck like we used to." But another part, a part I thought long healed, wanted to go where this was going, wanted revenge. Maybe Charley knew that, maybe he wanted it too. I obeyed.

Stepping back, I studied him, now spread-eagled before me. He pulled against the restraints, apparently judging the serious-ness of my participation. The muscles of his arms and shoul-ders bulged as he strained against the handcuffs. A trickle of sweat ran down his arm, darkening the edge of his tank top. I wanted to lick him, wanted to taste the salt on his skin. That realization drove blood straight up my cock. I was hard.

Charley gestured toward the bed with his chin. "Now go and get some nipple clamps."

I turned to the bed; laid out upon the gray sheet were implements I had only seen on porn sites: clamps, cock rings, a riding crop, items I didn't recognize. I picked up some clamps with jagged edges, like sharks' teeth.

"See that chain? Attach each of the clamps to the chain. Good. Now put them on me." He inhaled and his nipples pressed at the thin cloth of the shirt; already he was aroused. His breathing sharpened when I fastened the mean-looking pincers onto his chest. "Now twist." I gave each of the clamps a cautious turn.

"Harder!"

I hesitated, thinking of what Trey had done to Charley in school.

"Pull, you lazy bastard!"

His attitude raked at the scar tissue on my heart, angering me. I grabbed the chain and yanked hard, twisting his swollen nipples. I watched him squirm and arch his back; his body's reaction to the pain aroused me even more. I released the tension then pulled again and again. Charley groaned and panted, but said nothing.

Panting myself and frightened by my growing excitement, I let go of the chain. That obviously dissatisfied my old roommate.

"I love it," he sneered, a cruel smile playing across his lips. "They send a boy to do a man's work."

"What the fuck is that supposed to mean?"

"You heard me." Again our eyes met. The belligerent glare bore into me, picking at scabbed hurts. His aggression fanned my anger, really pissing me off. "Pussy."

I backhanded him, snapping his head to the side. "Enough of this shit!"

Turning back to face me, he licked at a smear of blood on his lip. That sight quelled my anger, and I wanted to comfort him, to stroke and soothe his face. But Charley laughed at the taste; the sound was cruel and stoked my rage again. He glanced down between us. "Look at my crotch, bud."

I followed his gaze. Beneath his khakis, his dick formed a ridge across his groin; a dime-sized circle of precome stained his right hip. He cocked his head, raising his reddening cheek toward me again.

"Come on, coward; do it! Hit me again!" Before he could repeat *coward*, he got it across the face. Twice I struck him—this time with my open palm. I'd hit him with such force, I knew that at least one side of his face would swell up soon. My palm smarted too. Charley continued to smile, leered at me even. "By the way—look at yourself."

I knew without looking: my own cock threatened to push out of my uniform.

"Admit it, Jake. This turns you on as much as it does me."

Shamed by my blatant arousal, I turned away. "God, you've become a bastard."

"We're not kids anymore, playing doctor with the lights out."

Growling my inarticulate humiliation and grief, I spun around and grabbed at his crotch. "You like fucking with people's minds, do you?" Grasping his balls, wanting to deflate the reproach of his erection, I yanked—hard. "Have you always liked screwing with their feelings?"

"Feelings?" he grunted. "Bullshit!"

I pulled harder. Charley gasped and didn't reply. Closing his eyes, he seemed to concentrate on the pain that must have throbbed through his gut and down his thighs.

"Was it just playing for you? Was it some sort of game?" I twisted his nuts and he moaned. "Was I just some dumb jock you manipulated into loving you?"

"I'm your prisoner," he deadpanned, unmoved by my admission.

Hurt and despair welled in my chest, firing the fury that burned within me. Letting go of his balls, I grabbed him by his hair, pulling his head close. "You were my lover!" My voice rasped; surging emotions threatened to choke me.

"Lover, ha!" He scoffed, spitting the words at me. "I'm your prisoner and I have information you want—and will get—if you have to beat it out of me."

Now I practically shook with rage. Reaching over to the bed, I picked up the biggest piece of leather I could lay my hand on. I raised it to his face.

"You're damn right I want information." I stroked the leather along his cheek, tracing the livid print of my hand along his jaw. "And I want you to give it to me now."

Charley panted, his shallow breaths wafting the smell of bourbon over me. "No."

"Yes, you will." My anger had mutated into a hard resolve. No longer did my hands shake when I caressed his neck with the piece of cowhide, following the rapid pulse of his jugular down to his chest. "I want you to tell me why you left." I flicked the leather against the clips that still chewed on his nipples.

His nostrils flared, but he gave no other sign of discomfort. "No," he whispered.

I moved the cowhide down his torso to press against his accusing hard-on. "Tell me why you deserted me without a single word. Not one word. Not one!" I smacked the leather against his khaki-covered thigh.

He gasped. "No."

"Tell me!" I whacked him again.

Licking his lips, he pursed them and swallowed. "No."

I beat the leather against his hips. He shook his head.

"Wasn't I worth at least a god...damned...good...bye?" Emphasizing each word with the leather, I struck him, swinging at his legs, his back and his butt.

Charley's body glistened, coated with his sweat. Mine poured from my forehead, running into my eyes, stinging them with salt. The longer he held out, the harder I hit him. A decade of pent-up frustration poured forth, became pure aggression against the man I had caressed and kissed in the dark. Now, under the bright, harsh light in this desolate, little room, I punished him for the pain he had caused me.

"Stop!" Charley cried out, breaking down at last. "I'll tell. Just wait."

I stopped, gulping air as my heart raced. Dropping the piece of leather, I grabbed his hair, gently this time. "I'm waiting," I panted.

To my surprise he leaned over and stuck his tongue in my mouth. We kissed deeply, our sweat mingling on our cheeks. Our lips and tongues entwined, each tasting the other as if for the first time. I ground my groin against his, wanting to fuck him.

He nuzzled my sweaty, beard-stubbled chin. "Forgive me... for holding out on you. I have a lot to tell."

"Go ahead." I nibbled on his earlobe.

"First, pull off my pants and grab a condom. I want you inside me."

Still cuffed to the cross, he grabbed hold of the chains and levered up his legs. I entered him, gripping the underside of his thighs. He rode me with his legs locked behind my back and humped his butt on my aching erection. He resembled a country boy on an old tire swing.

"I'm so sorry." He kissed my mouth. "I was so young. I was scared." He pulled me in close, impaling himself on my cock. "I wanted to forget it all ever happened. Everything. Even you."

"I loved you," I whispered in his ear, reveling in his musky scent. Still he stroked his ass on my cock.

"I loved you too." He licked my cheek. "But I was so hurt I couldn't even think about facing anybody or doing anything. Plus, I didn't want...how can I say this?"

I bit his neck. "Just say it."

He licked around my ear. "I didn't want anyone at school to know about you. I wanted to protect you. After all, you weren't a fag like me."

I pulled back and slowed the fucking. "Who do you think blew you at night?" My mouth found his again. "I was just as into it as you were."

"And you were great! And good for me. But..." He sucked on my tongue until I thought he'd pull it from my throat. "But... you never paid for it...the way I did."

I cradled him, carrying his weight the way I had that last night, a decade ago. "Did you ever talk about it? Get counseling or anything?"

He laughed a strained, taunting laugh. "Lots. You saw all that stuff!"

"What do you mean?"

"Look at the piece you grabbed." Charley kissed my forehead in a soft, feathery kiss.

Glancing down, I spotted the leather at my feet where I had discarded it. I had taken a razor strop from the bed. Probably identical to Trey's at the academy, the leather appeared alien and ugly to me. I felt weird—both repelled and turned on—and never closer to Charley.

"Don't stop fucking me," he urged, as if he sensed my withdrawal. He tenderly kissed my cheek. "It's you who's working me over now. You—the one I always loved." He tightened his hole on my cock. I swelled inside him. "Love me, fucker. Love me hard the way I need you to."

Our bodies entwined, our sweaty hips slapping together. Naturally, I obeyed him.

Later in the shower, Charley knelt before me and soaped up my legs, kissing my hips and drinking the water that ran in a thread off the head of my cock. The intimacy revived my hard-on.

I leaned against the wall, spent both physically and emotionally, yet never had I felt more alive. Charley picked up my left foot and lathered soap all over it. "I have one more thing to tell, but I'm scared you won't understand."

"Tell me anyway." I sighed, aware of nothing but the touch of Charley's fingers.

He kneaded and rubbed my toes, washing away my weariness with the suds. "About what happened with Trey. I was so ashamed because...because..."

I listened for an explanation. It was the least I could do.

"Because...I had sort of wanted him."

He waited for a response. I weighed the admission against my memories and remained silent.

Charley continued. "I always hated him—always. But I hated myself more." He moved to my right foot, lathering and caressing my toes. "I hated that I loved you and loved being with you, but, in spite of that, I was hot for him—all along."

I drew him up to face me. Tears streaked his face, little hidden by the spray. "I know. I probably always knew, even then. But I wasn't sure until tonight."

Charley rubbed his face; my handprint had begun to fade.

"The humiliation drove me away. That night you were so caring, so gentle, I couldn't bear to face you after that. I was sure that you'd see through me, see my ugly secret."

Taking him in my arms, I kissed him long and hard. "Now will you let the shame go?"

He grinned. "Do you mean it?" His relief lit up his eyes, brightening his face so much that I laughed too.

"Absolutely!" I bit his ear and spoke loud enough so that he would hear every word and never forget. "I am claiming my captive, and I am never going to release him."

He laughed, dousing our heads under the steamy spray. "Promise?"

"I promise. You're my prisoner."

SPLATTERDAYS

Steve Isaak

Jeremy sat at a small round table at the back of the midsized club, watching the mostly male metalheads mosh, thirty feet away. On the stage, the performing band, Dismembered By Cheetahs, aka DBC, raged out their trademark blend of chugging garage metal and raw-throated horror-flick lyrics.

The show was sold out; such was the popularity of the band, who'd arrived on the music scene in 1980, eleven years earlier. Sweat-soaked men and women, ages ranging from eighteen to fifty, brushed past Jeremy, hip-pushing at his hard wooden chair and occasionally bumping his table. He gripped his Guinness pint firmly.

The band ended their song, the staccato-edged "Choking on the Bile of Your Vile Unctiousness, Mom." The thrashers and those border-crushing around them stopped their smashing, dashing and headbanging, and were now standing still, dazed and happily exhausted.

Rigor Mortis, the dreadlocked lead vocalist, spoke into his

microphone. "Devilbong's original guitarist and one of our heroes, Brandon Page, died in a tragic accident eighteen years ago today. To mark the passing of this musical adept, Nub is going to play one of Page's solo tunes, 'An End to Friends.' We hope you like it."

Mortis nodded at Nub. The heavyset woman stepped up to her mic, smiled, and began to play a bluesy rock 'n' roll song on her guitar, sans vocals, as the spotlight singled her out.

Some of the audience members headed toward the bathroom, or toward the bar to get another drink or sit at one of the club's ten tables. As they pushed to the back of the club, the mingled odors of sweat, pot and cigarette smoke assaulted Jeremy's nose anew.

Jeremy smiled. Though he didn't smoke pot or cigarettes, these were his people. *Leather, band shirts and denim, all the way, baby*, he thought, mentally adding, *and the occasional handsome man who's great in the sack*.

There hadn't been much of the latter in his life, lately. He'd broken up with his last boyfriend, Paul, almost two months earlier. The reason: Paul, manager of a porn store, was working sixty-plus-hour weeks, with no reduction in sight. Paul had been irritable and emotionally abusive for the last few months of their relationship.

Jeremy, an easygoing person, didn't want the tension. So he split from the prick.

Paul hadn't taken Jeremy's move well. "We've been going out for almost a year, and because of a few arguments, you want to fuck other guys?" he'd yelled in their apartment.

"I don't want to 'fuck other guys,' and you know it," Jeremy had snapped back. "It's because you've been acting like a jerk for the last three months. I'm sorry that you're stressed out, and that your job sucks, but don't take it out on me, especially not in public. What you did at that party last night went too far!"

"You're overreacting," Paul had sneered. "Nobody said anything to me about it, besides you."

Jeremy took a deep breath. "Calling my opinions on writing 'fucking elitist and borderline retarded' in front of all our friends is scurrilous. Just because I prefer other horror writers over your beloved Dean Koontz doesn't mean I'm elitist. It means I have other preferences, that's all."

"'Scurrilous'?" Paul had mocked. "That's an elitist word. Who uses that word anymore?"

"People like me, who write every day, that's who. I'm not going to dumb myself down for your sorry ass, nor am I going to put up with your bullshit. We're through, Paul. I'm moving out tomorrow."

With that, Jeremy had gone to their bedroom, where he and Paul had spent many orgasmic and passionate hours, to pack a night bag for his motel stay.

The sound of a scraping chair drew Jeremy back to the present.

"Is it okay if I share this table with you?" asked a friendly male voice.

The body that packaged the voice was equally friendly—*fuckably friendly*, Jeremy thought, his senses electrified. His prick, which hadn't had much stimulation lately, aside from solo stroking, took notice too.

The hazel-eyed, twentysomething man looked amused, his right hand resting atop the back of the small wooden chair, his other holding a Guinness pint that mirrored Jeremy's. He wore a faded, edge-frayed Iron Maiden T-shirt, which clung, soaked, to his solid, buff body.

"Judging by your expression, the answer is yes?"

"Most definitely," Jeremy replied, softer than he meant to.

"Thank you," the stranger replied. He sat on the chair and set his pint on the table.

"I'm Adrian," he said, offering his hand.

Jeremy returned Adrian's smile and shook his hand. Though he'd thought he'd recovered from an initial shock of lust, Jeremy was rocked by further sexual energy when their hands touched.

He became aware that he was blushing while staring into Adrian's eyes. Adrian laughed politely, and said, "You never told me your name."

"Oh, sorry. I'm Jeremy."

"Glad to meet you, Jeremy." Adrian took in Jeremy's blond curls and blue eyes. Jeremy flushed again.

Adrian smiled. "You're a DBC fan?" He nodded at the stage, where Nub was finishing her cover song. The other band members had returned to the stage, and were taking their places; picking up their instruments: guitar, bass and drumsticks.

Jeremy nodded. "They broke my metal show cherry, back in '83, just before their first album came out."

"*Splatterday*. Fun album—not their best, but their punkiest."

"'Punkiest,'" Jeremy laughed. "I like that. May I use it?"

Adrian questioned him with a glance.

"I'm a writer," Jeremy explained.

"What do you write?"

"I scribble for a local rag, *The San Marin Weekly*."

Adrian smiled. "I've read that. What do you scribble about?"

"I mostly review local shows, new albums, and occasionally I interview visiting musicians. What do you do?"

"I'm a club employee. Got hired a few weeks ago. I'm a jack-of-all-trades assistant manager. And, yes, it's my night off."

Jeremy laughed. "Sounds like a cool job. Have you met anybody exciting?"

His question was interrupted by an eruptive, club-vibrating drumbeat from the stage.

Pukowski, bearded and sweaty on the drums, was kicking down a heavy bass beat, a familiar lead-in to one of DBC's live perennials, "Gethsemanic Maniacs," a song that hadn't appeared on any of their albums.

"Join me in the pit?" Adrian yelled, as he stood up and leaned down, inches from Jeremy's face.

Jeremy, wanting to kiss his beautiful mouth, blushed again. He ignored a knowing smile on Adrian's face.

Jeremy rose to join him, half hard, heart pounding.

By the time DBC ended its two-hour show with the corpse- and sex-nasty "Eat the Stiff Twitch," Jeremy and Adrian had "run the pit," as Jeremy called it, for five bruising, aching, blender-brutal songs.

Jeremy had managed to keep his erection manageable, or, as he called it, "non-raging," by *not* thinking about what Adrian might be like in bed. Not easy.

Besides, he wasn't a fast-fuck-and-run guy, even though Adrian was scathingly bangable. Jeremy, he learned, was twenty-six, liked relationships and had been in a few, all of them mostly good. There was something appealing about being with somebody you knew well, with whom you shared a wide array of experiences, some tender, some sad or angry, some funny, some sexual.

Adrian's tee was soaked again; Jeremy's was now, too. The thin cloth clung to their slender frames.

"You look flushed," Adrian said, slapping Jeremy lightly on the shoulder. "We should get something to drink—water, I mean."

Jeremy nodded, as they headed toward the club exit. "My throat's dry. And I'm drenched."

Adrian grinned at the play on words, and Jeremy, silently cursing, blushed again.

"Nice blush. I find you attractive, too," Adrian said. "I'd like to go out on a date with you. A real date, not *this*." With a wave of his right hand, Adrian indicated the club around them.

"That would be good." Jeremy smiled.

On their third date in less than two weeks—dinner at a vegetarian restaurant—Adrian told Jeremy about his last boyfriend, Gary, who'd quite literally pulled a disappearing act on him.

"All he left was a stupid note," Adrian snorted. "It read: *I have to go. Please don't look for me. Know, however, that I will always love you.* That was almost a year ago. What kind of shit is that?"

"Are you over him?"

Adrian thought a moment, smiled. "Yeah. I'm not pining for him, but the mystery of his disappearance—and, yes, I looked for him—is still weird."

Adrian paused again and looked Jeremy in the eye. "I didn't really answer your question, did I? The answer is yes, I'm ready for another relationship, a monogamous one. Possibly with you, if things work out."

"And if they didn't work out?" Jeremy smiled.

"We'll get some sweet lovemaking out of it," Adrian said flirtatiously.

"My, my. So forward for someone who hasn't bedded me yet," Jeremy laughed. He continued to blush around Adrian, but not as much, thank god.

"You said 'yet.'"

"Okay, how about right now," Jeremy said, leaning forward

and French-kissing Adrian in the middle of the busy restaurant.

Ignoring an elderly woman's gasp, Adrian surrendered to Jeremy's oral heat. This wasn't their first kiss, but it was their most passionate.

They broke away from each other.

"My place?" Jeremy asked, quietly, his gaze intense.

"Of course. It's closer." Adrian laughed.

Fifteen minutes later, they were at Jeremy's apartment.

Jeremy barely had time to unlock his front door before Adrian, his kisses flavored by Guinness Stout, gently pushed him inside, kicking the door shut with his foot.

They slammed against a hallway wall, quaking—almost knocking down—a framed photo of an adolescent Jeremy with his parents, all of them smiling.

Their hands fumbled with, unbuttoned, tugged off their clothes, their kisses rough: Jeremy reveled in the soft facial chafing of Adrian's three-day beard and his sandalwood-scented skin, as Adrian, who'd divested Jeremy of his pants and boxers, insistently kissed his way down to Jeremy's aching-to-burst erection.

He had barely put his prick into Adrian's hot, wet mouth when he came, gasping.

Adrian, lusty gentleman that he was, worked Jeremy's member, his hands gently squeezing Jeremy's sac. Dizzy with desire, Jeremy spasmed even more as he leaned back against the wall.

A minute later, Adrian rose from his knees. His Guinness kisses were now flavored with Jeremy's salty nut.

Jeremy sighed. "Sorry for coming so quickly."

"Don't apologize," Adrian said, his eyes bright, between further kisses. "Take me to your bed."

Inside Jeremy's bedroom, Jeremy did as Adrian bid. They

continued making out, their hands stroking, squeezing each other's taint, prick and sac till both had fresh erections.

Jeremy broke away for a few seconds to riffle for his lube and condoms in his nightstand. Even as he did this, he traced circular patterns on Adrian's solid, lightly haired stomach with the fingers of his other hand, occasionally brushing them against the tip of Adrian's raging red prick.

"Hurry," Adrian said, that he was on the brink of coming apparent in his voice. "I'm going to explode, if you don't."

"Then explode," Jeremy sighed, loudly dropping his lube jar and strung-together condoms on the nightstand. He scooted down the bed and slowly tongued the head of Adrian's prick.

"You tasted me, now I want to taste you," he said, sweaty and breathing hard, almost as hard as Adrian. "It's only fair."

Adrian, clutching the sheets, arched slightly when he came, the taste bitter-tinged, in his lover's mouth.

A moment later, Adrian sighed, "Thank you. I needed that."

"I should be thanking *you*," Jeremy said, wiping Adrian's come from the corner of his mouth while he scooted up to rest his head on the other pillow and face Adrian.

Adrian smiled. "We're both lucky. Good night, lover."

"What about the lube, the condoms?" Jeremy asked, mock-distressed.

"There'll be plenty of other opportunities to rock that sweetness. Say…all day tomorrow?"

Jeremy nodded, any words thick, stuck in his throat.

"Good," Adrian said, then promptly fell asleep, leaving Jeremy to gaze lovingly at him for much of the remaining night.

The next morning, they made beautiful music together—and it wasn't all heavy metal—again. And for a long time to come.

PRECIOUS JADE

Fyn Alexander

I was beautiful in 1885 when Queen Victoria was on the throne, and I still am, according to someone who loves me. I was paid far more attention than I deserved by both men and women, and was, frankly, rather vain. At eighteen years old I was slender with sun-colored hair that was much too long and skin like an unblemished peach.

I had grown up in the theatre as an angelic boy soprano. But, much to my chagrin, my voice changed at fourteen, and along with it, my ability to earn a living. Consequently, that warm day in May the very thought of having to attend an interview for a job I did not want at a house in Belgravia made me as sullen as a spoiled prince.

Money I wanted, a place to live I needed, but work! I wanted to cry out to God to save me. Why could I not be rich and free and live in some foreign clime where it was always warm and no one cared that I, a boy, preferred men to ladies? I favored girls when it came to chitchat, gossip and whispering about men's bodies. But I had always wanted a man to overpower me, to master me, to fall madly in love with me and make me his own. Since I was to be a servant of sorts, a secretary, you would think I'd be happy, but no! Any master I would end up with would be either some doddering old man I did not want near me, or some nasty married gentleman who would treat me with utter disdain, if he noticed me at all.

It wasn't fair.

I suppose I must have looked disgruntled when I was shown into the study and made to stand in front of a broad oak desk whilst being looked up and down by an elderly woman dressed in black silk. She never invited me to sit. She fired questions at me while acting as if I had brought a smell of refuse into the house with me. All in all, I felt like reaching across the desk to slap her cadaverous cheek. I found my left eyebrow lifting as it often did when I was affronted. Remembering my mother's admonition before I left that morning—"Keep that haughty look off your face, darling boy. An employer will not take kindly to it"—I lowered my eyebrow and attempted to look meek.

"Your mother is on the stage? She calls herself Amethyst Swift?" Mrs. Wynterbourne asked. From her tone she might as well have said, *Your mother is a prostitute, she has sex for money with perfect strangers.*

"My mother is a singer, a coloratura, and that's her *real* name." My eyebrow shot up again of its own volition.

"And she extended the family tradition of naming infants after stones by calling you Jade?" She actually sniggered, a very unattractive sound.

I was outraged. I clasped my hands behind my back to control them. "Jade is very expensive. It is the same color as my eyes." The first man who had ever taken me on his knee and petted me had told me my green eyes were *fit to die in.*

"Is it indeed?" Mrs. Wynterbourne's eyebrows both rose perilously close to her receding hairline. "Watch your tone, my lad! Why are you not on the stage yourself? You might be better suited to that life." She was obviously referring to my long hair and velvet jacket.

"My mother wants something better for me," I said quietly, ashamed to admit it.

"Does she indeed? Well, I suppose the job is yours."

"Thank you," I muttered, taken by surprise. The sun shone through the window behind her directly into my eyes, making me hot and crotchety. I wanted desperately to get away from her. "May I see my room please? Then I can go and fetch my belongings."

"You will not be staying here," she said as if the very thought was repugnant to her. "You are going to the country to work for my son, Mr. Marcus Wynterbourne, who fancies he is writing a book. He wants me to send him a young lady, but I don't trust him with one."

Not to be trusted with young ladies? Just my luck!

The journey to East Sussex on the public coach was hellish, to say the least. Squashed in for the first half of the journey between a fat, dirty woman and her farting husband, then for the second leg, alone in the carriage with a man with roving hands and halitosis, my senses were outraged along with my very person. The first I ignored as best I could: the second I slapped, then bit when he refused to accept my firm refusal.

I arrived eventually in the pitch dark at a vast country estate, tired, hungry, dejected and wanting my mother. None of my needs were met except for a bed, and I retired hungry and miserable, bursting into tears under the covers. Sometime later I paused in my pathetic weeping, swearing I heard a step outside my door. I drew the eiderdown up under my chin like a maiden defending her virtue, though my virtue was long since trampled upon, and I was more disappointed than anything when no one entered my lonely chamber.

Over breakfast with the servants, who never spoke directly to me, and looked at me as though I were a recent escapee from a traveling freak show, I fantasized about my new Master as I had done since first hearing his name: Marcus Wynterbourne. Since childhood I had dreamed of a man, cold and haughty, whose icy heart could only be melted by me. But Mr. Wynterbourne liked the ladies, it seemed, and he was probably ugly anyway.

At length I was shown into a sunny morning room, where a man stood at the window with his back to the room, ignoring me. I remained standing by the door until he deigned to turn around. When at last he did, the sight of him captured my breath as I had dreamed it would.

When he approached me, I observed a man nearly as slender as myself, though far taller and more masculine. He had black hair beginning to be streaked with silver, intense dark eyes and a frenetic presence. I stepped back, afraid for a moment he would grab me to examine me more closely. Instead he pulled a letter from his pocket and held it at arms' length to read it. "James Swift," he pronounced. "Eighteen years old, well read, handwriting excellent."

"Jade," I corrected. "Sir, my name is Jade Swift."

He laughed, an almost frightening sound, then stopped abruptly. "Jade? My mother changed your name. She wants you to be James while you work for me." He looked me up and down, a sarcastic smile playing about his mouth.

"Well, I won't be," I said, petulantly. I had had quite enough. "My name is Jade. I insist upon it." My heart fluttered as I spoke.

"Do you?" He stepped closer, looking down at me. He really was very tall.

"Yes, Sir," I whispered, not quite so sure of myself now that I could feel his breath against my cheek. He smelled wonderful, nothing fancy, just expensive, masculine soap and a splash of Bay Rum. He was clean-shaven in a time when whiskers on a man were all the rage. I could not admit him handsome with his strong jaw and thin face. In fact he was a bit scary looking. However, it would not be a lie to call him attractive.

"Jade," he said, as if mocking me. "I am writing a book and you will take dictation and fetch any volumes I require for my research, though most of my writing is a memoir of my extensive travels. Go to my office at the end of the hall and wait there for me."

As I trotted down the carpeted hall I experienced a violent excitement in my stomach. *Love at first sight* is what they call it, and a romantic boy like myself had passed many a happy hour envisioning such an event. I had felt attraction at first sight so many times it did not bear scrutiny. Indeed, there were times when a wink from a pretty boy or handsome man was sufficient to have me following him like a puppy into the first dark corner available. But this weakness of the stomach, this unfathomable desire, was new to me. Several minutes later my Master entered the room, threw himself into the chair behind the desk and began to dictate.

That was it for the next month and a half. He dictated while I transcribed. He ignored me completely while I sat bored stiff and longing to be noticed. He marched up and down the room speaking into the air, hands clasped behind his back. I caught my breath every time he walked too close, which he did increasingly as the weeks passed until I was driven insane with yearning. I entered my room each evening, my cheeks drenched in tears of frustration, to write a missive to mother about how desperate I was for London, the Theater and her.

I was completely infatuated with my Master and I had a suspicion that he knew. I had a great tendency to fall easily in and out of love, and every time I did, I thought it would last forever. But what I was beginning to feel for Mr. Wynterbourne was different. The usual intense emotions were there, but it was as if something deep-rooted had begun to grow inside me. I sought a communion with him I did not understand and could not have put into words even if I had wanted to.

One afternoon he leaned over my shoulder so closely that his body touched mine and said, "Let me see what you have so far, boy." The feel of his warm breath against my ear caused my cock to rise. I swear he chuckled as he walked back to his desk. Sometime in early July he caught me distracted and staring out into the grounds, which had grown beautiful with the fullness of summer. I had missed several lines of dictation.

"Am I keeping you from something you would rather be doing, boy?" His sarcastic schoolmaster tone snatched me from my reverie. I turned to him, my ire raised. I was sick of the job and sick of pining for a kind word or a warm look from him. I would rather he slapped me than offer this total negation of my being.

"I should never have left London!" I burst out like a ridiculous child.

Very calmly he asked, "What would you have done had you remained?" With one hand, he pulled the chair from behind his desk, plumped it in the middle of the room and sprawled in it, elbows propped on the arms, fingers steepled, long legs stretched out before him. His intense gaze rested upon me and my cheeks began to grow warm. The only thing I hated about being so blond was the tendency for every emotion to show in my face. He beckoned me to stand before him. "Speak," he demanded. "Tell me all about yourself."

I was in shock. Moments ago I was bored to tears and resentful that he ignored me. Now I stood before him, all his attention focused on me, and I wished myself a mile hence. I had no idea where to start. "My mother is on the stage. I too worked on the stage."

"What did you do on the stage?" His eyes looked serious yet his mouth tilted at the corners and I was certain he wanted to laugh.

"I was a magician's assistant for a time and sometimes I would dress up to take part in skits, but I want to be a singer again. I sang on the stage when I was younger. I was billed as *Amethyst's Angel*. But then my voice broke."

"That does tend to happen. Sing for me," he ordered.

I trembled. I stood only a few feet from him utterly exposed in this small venue. I clasped my hands before me and raised my voice in an old music hall love song. When I was done the silence filled the room with far more intensity than my singing.

At last he spoke. "Why did you leave the theater?"

"My mother insisted I do something more respectable." I hated saying that, but it was what she told me.

"Your mother wanted you to do something you could make a living at because you will never again make a living with that voice. It's awful," he said calmly.

I turned from him quickly to hide the hot tears coursing down my pink cheeks. I hated him! I wanted to strike him and run from the house back to my mother. How could he treat me so cruelly?

"Boy," I heard him say. I would not face him again, but stood at the window with heaving shoulders, crying silently. Then he was behind me, wrapping a strong arm around my waist, pinning my body to his. With his other hand he wiped my tears and drew me round to face him. I pressed my hot face into his chest and felt his hand on the back of my head, caressing my hair.

"Jade. Precious Jade," he whispered my name. "Don't cry, beautiful boy." Thrilled and shocked by turns at this unexpected intimacy, I dared not move for fear he would become sensible of his madness and let me go. "Your voice is dreadful but I was rather cruel in saying so. Your writing on the other hand is excellent. You take fast dictation and your skill at research is impressive. You are a clever boy. Well spoken and with a fine vocabulary."

"Thank you, Sir," I replied through my tears, thrilled at the praise, yet still feeling limp and stupid.

"I have grown very fond of you," he said quietly. Then he held me at arm's length, gazing down at me. "And you are beautiful."

I was so confused. For weeks he had been distant, calling me Swift or boy, mostly boy. Now he called me precious Jade and held me in his arms. Was he toying with me? I threw myself at him and wrapped my arms around his waist as if I would never let him go. "Sir, Mrs. Wynterborne said you are not to be trusted around young ladies," I ventured. "Yet I have never seen a lady in your company."

"Yes, I know. It is me who belongs on the stage, not you, boy. I'm a fine actor. But what choice do we have?" He smiled kindly for the first time in all those weeks and his voice was tender when he said, "May I have you?"

I nearly fainted. Was it really that simple? Had he really just offered to make me his own, or had I misheard? "Yes, please, Sir," I said without hesitation, assuming he would sweep me up in his arms and carry me to his bedchamber, much to the shock and horror of any servant we passed on the way.

My Master was a very strong man despite his slender build, possessing tight, sinewy muscles, and now he put his strength to good use. Before I could react, he had my trousers down and threw me over the back of a chair.

It seemed the virtue I thought I had lost long ago was still intact, because I had never dreamed of what he did to me next. I was an innocent. I was a virgin! All my kissing and fumbling in various cobwebby corners of London theaters was nothing but childish play, preamble to this moment. Mr. Wynterbourne reamed me good and proper, then fastened his trousers and sat down again behind his desk. I turned to look at him, myself still in dishabille, and he merely started to dictate again. Utterly humiliated, I dragged up my trousers, grabbed my pen and ink and attempted to keep up.

That night in bed, I cried my heart out. Master had pretended to want me, then he had done no more than use me like a piece of meat from Smithfield Market. My sobbing was so loud and indulgent that I did not hear him enter my room. At some point I looked up to find him standing silently beside my bed. I sat up at once and did the eiderdown thing again, which made him laugh. "You're cruel!" I burst out, and began to weep once more, before crying, "I love you." How pathetic I must have sounded.

"Yes," he agreed. "Of course you love me. I expected you would the moment I saw you with your peach-perfect skin and overly long hair." He cocked his head to one side, looking down at me from his great height. Then he sat on my bed and took my trembling hands in his. "Do you wish to be my boy, precious Jade?"

I drew his hands to my mouth, smothering them with kisses. "Yes, Sir, yes please, Sir."

Solemnly, he nodded. "I knew you would accept." Had he been anybody else I would have wanted to teach him a lesson for being so smug. But he was not anybody else. He was my Master. All I felt was gratitude and a desperate desire to please him.

Disappointment flooded me when he stood and walked to the door. I thought at least he would invite me to his chamber. "Be prompt in my office in the morning as usual and in the evening we will talk about my expectations for your new position."

My confusion must have been obvious; still, he waited for me to ask. "New position, Sir? I am still working for you, aren't I?"

"You will continue as my secretary," he agreed. "Indeed, I could not do without you for my book. But now you are more than that. Now you are my slave."

"Yes, Sir, thank you, Sir," was all I could say.

The next morning I reported for my day's work in Master's study, my heart pounding. I expected him to greet me with a kiss and an embrace. He did not. As always, he waited for me at his desk, and the moment I entered the room, he pointed at my escritoire. I sat down, and he began to dictate before I could pick up my pen.

All night I had hardly slept, sick with anticipation and excitement, and for what? This? Being ignored as usual. Being treated like a piece of furniture as usual. As the day wore on, so did my unease. Had I imagined him coming to my chamber last night? Had I wanted him so desperately that I had imagined the entire scene?

At six o'clock, just as I thought he would have me writing far into the evening, Mr. Wynterbourne stopped speaking and walked to the window. I watched him stand silent for a while, and then he looked at me with his intense gray eyes. "Come here, boy."

In my excitement to get to him, I dropped my pen to the floor, then moaned in fear that I had splattered ink onto the beautiful Persian rug. I stooped to pick it up, fumbling stupidly, and returned it to the pen case. He watched, smiling, and waited patiently until I stood before him. I wanted to throw myself at him but dared not presume.

He held out his arms to me, and I fell into them with such relief that I feared I might weep again. "Sir, I thought you had changed your mind," I mumbled into his lapel.

"Not at all, dear boy. When I decide upon something, I always know I have made the right decision."

My instructions were rather simpler than I had expected. My Master said, "Obey me in everything. Obey me at once. I will always be fair with you. I will never let anyone hurt you. Be humble and be proud at the same time. Do you find that confusing? Don't worry, boy. I will show you what I mean. Nothing will be expected of you that is beyond your ability to achieve."

Later that week they came, the men and women of The Hellfire Club. Never in my short life had I beheld such an assemblage as gathered in the drawing room that evening, and I had grown up in the theater! I had seen boys dressed as girls and girls dressed as boys. I had met a good number of both ladies and gentlemen who preferred their own sex to the other. My mother had a friend who was born with two penises, which he insisted on showing me one evening, and I must confess I was fascinated. But these people who knew, and clearly loved, my Master, took the cake.

Whilst the butler served brandy, which I was not offered, I was ordered to sit on the carpet at my Master's knee. I felt the great weight of this honor and was frankly rather smug about it. *Do they all know I'm his,* I wondered. It seemed they did because a number of very haughty men and women looked down on me and asked, "Is this your new boy, Marcus? Isn't he pretty."

At one point I responded, "Yes, I'm Jade Swift," and received a slap across the back of my head for my trouble.

"The only thing swift from now on will be retribution if you speak again without permission," Master told me firmly. Burning with humiliation I learned a sharp lesson, the first of many, and sat in silence eyeing the party.

The Masters and Mistresses were unmistakable because they walked about freely or sat on the beautiful furniture while talking and laughing. Many wore clothing that designated some sort of rank—heavy, leather belts with metal studs and high leather boots. More than that it was their attitude, the authority with which they carried themselves, that set them apart from their minions.

The slaves, though, sat on the floor, some naked under their cloaks and with various chains and restraints upon their persons. They were silent unless spoken to, kept their eyes lowered for the most part, and remained very still beside their Masters and Mistresses. I became fascinated by a man, quite a bit older than myself and wearing what appeared to be a muzzle, who sat beside a woman's knee, panting like a dog and suffering constant, exacting correction. I looked up at Master, and when he noticed me, I nodded at them. He leaned down, saying, "That is a puppy in training."

My mind was in a whirl.

Soon enough I followed my Master and his guests down into the extensive cellars of the great house. A sign on an immense barred wooden door read DUNGEON, and my heart began to pound. The dungeon was lit by flaming torches set in wall sconces. The corners were dark and cavernous. There was a general air of revelry; the slaves bright-eyed, their chests heaving; the Masters and Mistresses sure of themselves and in control.

I was ordered to strip as were all the slaves, male and female, young and old and every age between. Master, who dazzled my eyes in his black trousers, black leather boots and snow-white shirt, watched me and smiled as my nipples and cock reacted to the cool air.

"Precious Jade, tonight you will be tested," he said. Overwhelmed with excitement, I was led to a post by the wall where I was bound like Christ on the cross, ankles together, hands above my head. I was a picture of angelic beauty with my blond hair about my shoulders and my slender body stretched out for all to admire. And admired I was for about five minutes by my Master's friends, gathered about to gaze at me. It was my moment in the spotlight. Then it was over. "Observe everything, beautiful boy," were Master's last words to me. After that I was left alone.

For the remainder of the night I witnessed scenes that enthralled and delighted me, yet I was miserable. I went from boredom to tears of frustration, from horror to fascination as the hours wore on. From my ignominious place in a dark corner I watched floggings and spankings that I wanted to experience. I saw slaves restrained and gagged in a myriad of different positions and styles, with everything from rope to leather thongs to iron manacles, and I was jealous. I saw hot wax poured over sensitive body parts making me wince while wanting to experience the sensation. I saw a life I wanted and I was provoked to insane jealousy of every slave my Master touched, flogged, punished or smiled upon.

When at long last my Master came over to me. I wanted to scream at him in frustration, but I was clever enough to know that that would be a mistake. "Master, you said you would test me," I said quietly.

"You have been tested, precious Jade." With care he released me from my bonds. "Your patience has been tested and you have made me proud." I all but swooned with joy. He took my face in his hands. "You are an impatient, demanding boy and I am going to tame you. Everything is a lesson. Now come with me." He led me to the middle of the dungeon and to my delight spanked me soundly while everyone watched. I was in the spotlight again.

Afterward he hugged me close and I whispered, "I love you, Sir," and waited for him to respond likewise. But all he said was, "And so you should. You should always love your Master."

In the days that followed I learned that I held a cherished place in my Master's heart. While he was teaching me the basics of being his slave I was showered with praise, kisses, scrumptious hours in the dungeon—and my favorite thing in the world—the privilege of being allowed to sit in Master's lap. At night I was permitted to sleep beside him in his bed. But he never declared his love for me, if he had any.

I began to get quite full of myself, I admit. The euphoria I experienced from being tested to the limits of my endurance can only be compared with the heightened awareness I got from sharing my Master's best opium, which on a few rare occasions I was allowed, and which I sometimes thought made me invincible.

It was this invincibility which led me to thinking it my right to take advantage of an offer from a handsome, sun-browned gardener, only a little older than myself, whose sole desire one hot afternoon was to suck my admittedly small cock behind the stables. He was on his knees and I had my eyes tight shut, moaning openly when I felt the stinging flick of a whip across my bare belly. My eyes shot open. My handsome friend screamed as he too took a lash from Master's single tail, across his bare back. The pair of us stood with our heads hung like schoolboys before an enraged headmaster. The gardener was sent back to his duties whimpering after several more lashes and I was slapped hard across the cheek and ordered to pack my bags.

* * *

In the days that followed, in my mother's dingy lodgings, I poured out the whole tale of passionate love and delicious subjugation. Mother held me close in her big bed at night while I sobbed for all I had lost. I pressed my face into her ample bosom and was able to keep my sobs down to merely pathetic while she stroked my long hair, twisting it into ringlets round her finger, saying "Mother's darling boy." It was when she called me her *precious Jade*, my sobs rose to truly melodramatic heights. "He calls me that!" I wailed.

I had always thought a broken heart was something to aspire to, something that would set a boy apart, making him purer and nobler. I never expected a broken heart would leave me weak and empty. Snot dribbled down my face as I sobbed; I pissed in my mother's bed two nights in a row. She forgave me, god bless her, but after a week she told me in no uncertain terms that there was a job available at the Adelphi Theatre cleaning the dressing rooms and that I had better take it and bring in some money.

I was humiliated to the very core of my being after my first day as a broom boy. I lay thoroughly exhausted, curled up in the middle of mother's bed, watching her ready herself to go back there to "warble for the punters," as she put it.

"Visitor!" was screamed up the stairs by the landlady whenever one arrived. I did not move from my prone position, not expecting anyone would want to see me. Mother opened the door and invited the visitor in.

"Get up when I enter a room, boy." I heard my Master's voice and reacted like a starved dog. I leapt to my feet, stumbled to my knees and kissed his black leather boots. Mother raised her eyes to the damp-stained ceiling, proclaiming, "Good god," and sat down again to arrange her hair. "If your intention was to humble my sweet boy, you've done it. Now will you please take him back?" she said calmly.

I sat back on my heels waiting for his answer, looking up into the face I had grown to love and had missed desperately these empty days. I waited, afraid to breathe. "How do I know he is sufficiently humbled?" Master asked.

Mother swung around on her stool. She was in her silk corset and lace-edged pantaloons, her face half made up, and was not the slightest bit abashed by my fine gentleman. "He cries for you every night. He calls out your name in his sleep. He hardly eats." *Please don't tell him I pissed in the bed*, I thought desperately. "And he wet my bed the first two nights he was home," she added for good measure.

I hung my head in shame.

"Excellent," Master stated, smiling at mother. "I see where the boy gets his beauty."

Mother was not averse to flattery even from a lover of men, and smiled back. "Too bad he didn't get my voice. He has the face of an angel and he used to sound like one, but the minute he turned fourteen..." She shook her head sadly.

"Yes, I've heard him sing," Master said. They continued talking as though I were absent.

"What made you come to get him back?" Mother asked.

I gazed up at Master adoringly, wanting him to say, *I miss him, I love him, I need him.* Instead he said, "I always intended to come for him. This was just another lesson. I could have flogged his bare arse until he screamed as a punishment for taking liberties, but I thought the gentler way might be better on this occasion." He looked down at me, wagging a finger. "Pack your bag and come home. And this time, behave yourself."

"Do you love me, Master?" I whispered. "Do you love me as I love you?"

After a long pause, during which mother turned her back to allow us a modicum of privacy in the small room, Master said loudly and firmly, "Yes, Jade, I love you. I love you very much."

I smothered his boots with kisses and still do whenever I am overcome with gratitude that Master noticed me all those years ago when I was eighteen years old, presumptuous and foolish. He still calls me his *precious Jade* and he still tells me I am beautiful.

FROM A JOURNEY

Håkan Lindquist

*Did you imagine one day the sun would not rise, that
I would be left to bear witness to our friendship?*
—Derek Jarman, *Derek Jarman's Garden*

My first impression of you, Daniel. Do you remember?

You arrive at the cliff an hour or so after me. I'm already lying naked in the sun, listening to the clicking as you lock your bike, listening to your footsteps—at first dull in the moss beside the path, then clearer as you reach the rock—and I'm slowly turning to see who you are. *Who are you?*

Your dark hair is ruffled by the wind. The sunlight is dancing off your white T-shirt and dazzles me. I lift my hand to shade my eyes and I look directly into yours. You smile. I don't really dare to respond. And so you undress—the boots, the shorts, the T-shirt. Ritually.

You are lying in the sun in the center of my sight. I guess there is seventeen feet between us. If I put out my left arm as far as I can, it's only fourteen feet. And if you would reach out your right arm... Do you realize we could be getting even closer to each other?

An hour or so later: my eyes have followed you, followed your steps. You are not really tiptoeing but you mainly use the front part of your feet as you walk to the water. Now you are returning to your place on the cliff. But then something happens. You turn toward me. You are getting closer, now you're really close, and you say something.

"Sorry?" I stutter.

"The water was warmer two weeks ago."

You squat, and I clearly see your eyes, your lips, your cheek, drops of water glittering on your body.

I mumble something. Do you remember what? I no longer do.

Then you stand. You fold your arms across your chest, under-lining the small silver object on the chain around your neck. It is the first day of our mutual life. It is the first day of our mutual journey, as far as we know. I don't think I've seen you before. You don't remember seeing me before. And while I'm following the smooth lines of your body and noticing its fantastic details, you suddenly shiver and go all goose-pimply. And I am in love. Do you realize that, Daniel? I am already in love with you, with us. In love.

Several years earlier

Eric is sitting at one of the long tables at the club. I am standing with my back against the raised dance floor with a beer in my hand. The music is throbbing through me. Hanging from the ceiling is a rotating globe of mirrors that, in a fragmented form, reflects everything and everyone. But all I see is him. Eric. And so he turns and smiles. I smile back, lifting my glass, thinking I am—no, knowing I am—in love.

Shortly thereafter Eric comes up to me, asking me for a dance. Of course we shall dance. And his light curls bounce in a dance of their own as we move over the floor. All the time I'm smiling, and I can't take my eyes off his face, his mouth, his lips...

It is late at night or early morning on the street where he lives. The two windows in his bedroom are open to the dark and the January cold. As the bell tolls in the twin-towered church, we take off our clothes. Your, no, *his* white shirt has been stained at one of the collar tips. My white shirt smells of cigarettes. I am watching his naked body. He is almost as skinny as me, and his chest is slighter. His nipples are dark brown, small and beautiful. It is our first day together and my hand is shaking as I reach out to touch him.

The seventh time we made love, Daniel, do you remember? The morning after we woke up, realizing it was the anniversary of Eric's death. Eight years. And I dare to say you remind me of Eric. Yes, I even dare to put another thought into words: you and I are continuing a journey that Eric and I started on one January night years ago. And you, Daniel, say *we* are out on a particular journey. You must remember. All of a sudden I feel much more present, more alive, and the years that have passed since the death of Eric and our first meeting on the cliff seem like a dark room that is getting brighter. And the journey continues. Do you realize I would very much like to use that big word love when I'm trying to explain what I feel for you, Daniel, but I don't really dare. Some words are just too big.

I stayed in the bathroom after you had gone. The mirror over the washbasin was following my movements. I spit out the toothpaste, put the brush in its place, and met my reflected eyes. I tried to see those things you saw when you were watching me, but I wasn't really sure what they were, though it suddenly struck me that I'm very pleased that you think me beautiful.

The next day I take my bike to the cliff.

"Daniel," I whisper to myself as I park the bike against the huge pine tree by the path. And then, once again, "Daniel," as I leave the path and cross the rock to look for a space among all those men, all those bodies that aren't you.

I'm lying on my stomach after my second swim in the bay. The water is warm again. A small breeze stirs it and the reeds by the cliff side rustle in harmonious lamentation with my thoughts.

The sun is blazing down on my back.

It was very hot the summer Eric died, hotter than it had been for years. I had a long vacation and I was swimming and spending most of my time in the sun. I was a long way from home, the sun was blazing down on my back, and the sky was as clear and blue as a picture postcard. How could I ever have guessed what was to happen? Surely no one would die on a day like this? Do you remember how much I loved you, Eric? Can you remember how it felt when I was touching you? Can you still feel my fingers?

I wake up on the cliff.

The wind is stronger and the reeds are even more upset. They call out sadly as the wind forces them to bend. Their voices reach me and I suddenly feel a tremendous desire for your hands on my body, Daniel, and my hands on yours.

I think of you, of us. Of the two of us making love. I imagine myself being strong, lifting you up, steadily and firmly, turning you over and whispering, *"Ephphatha! Ephphatha!"* [*Be opened...*] I come inside you while you sigh in that moving, irresistible way that is yours alone. Your left hand glides back and forth over the mattress, as if looking for something to touch, something to hold. I would very much like to kiss the back of your neck, the soft and curly hair there, to inhale your scent, to whisper to you all the emotions I feel, all the sensations I wish for. You know them already, you've heard them so often. In spite of the fact that it's just two weeks since our first meeting on the cliff, we've already said so much. With and without words. But I tell you all this once again. My grandmother says: "What's important is worth repeating." I've heard her say it a hundred times.

The things I write to you are important, Daniel. The things I tell you are important.

The sun is still blazing and I am dazed as I stumble down to the water for a final dip. Have I forgotten anything? Any unrepeated thing? Of course I have. And therefore I will have to write to you again, talk to you again, Daniel. Repetitions and additions. What's important is worth repeating.

I think of your body as the refreshing water closes around me. Your chest, your beautiful chest...the soft *V*-shape that so gracefully holds the outline of your ribs. Your nipples, so unlike mine, so unlike Eric's. I desire touching, being touched. Do you, Daniel, believe I love you?

The wind is cold now. I shiver as I come out of the water. There are many men on the cliff, but I don't want to talk with them. I don't want them to talk to me. Soon I'll be on my way home, longing.

My lips, my hands, my ears, my eyes, my chest, my nose, my legs, my stomach, my bottom, my dick, my arms, my long back... Every part suffers from abstinence, every part longs for closeness. Daniel-closeness.

Now the reeds are bent over.

* * *

Eric's mother died when he was eleven years old. She had been ill for a very long time, which to him must have seemed like an eternity.

We were lying in the inherited dark-brown oak bed at Eric's house. The morning sun was shining through the window, but the light had not yet reached the bed.

"What are you thinking of, Eric?"

He was still and silent, watching the light as it reached the green-painted box we used as a bedside table. The light made it shimmer in a peculiar way. On top of the box stood a photo of his mother.

"What are you thinking of, Eric?"

"The last time I left my mother I slammed the door after me. I was angry 'cause she didn't give me something I wanted. So I yelled at her and left without saying good-bye. I just slammed the door."

By now the light had reached the photograph. The silver frame was sparkling, the glass protecting the picture reflected the strong light, preventing us from seeing her face.

"There is always a last time," I said carefully, "but that doesn't mean it is the only occasion that counts, the only moment that matters. You must have shared many good moments with your mother."

Now he was close to crying.

"Yes, of course," he replied, his voice almost inaudible. "I know. But I still feel bad when I think about it."

I was lying on my side, resting my left hand on his chest. Under my palm, I could feel his heart beating.

I hesitated, then said:

"Sometimes when we are lying here I can sense her presence. It's as if she's here, supporting us. As if she is giving us her consent, her approval. I feel it quite often."

There were tears in Eric's eyes, but he was smiling.

"I know," he whispered. "I know."

We are making love. And once again, a church bell accompanies our passionate breathing. But this time it's us, Daniel. This time it's you and me. It's our breathing, our journey. And the bell is one of the bells in the church near where I live. You often say the quarters seem shorter at my place.

My fingers are playing inside you. I like to warm my fingers in you, Daniel. I like to listen to the soft whimpers my movements conjure up in you. I like to see your eyes shaded by lust, by love. I very much like to make love with you, Daniel, to know all your scents.

Afterward we are lying like twins watching the soft light that has found its way into my room and is entertaining us on the ceiling.

"My apartment is different when you're here," I say. "Everything's the same, but more so. Like when it's cloudy outside and the colors are clearer than usual."

You are smiling. And the light in the room is in your eyes, causing them to shine.

I turn to rest on my side, my left hand caressing your chest, your stomach, your scrotum. Now it's resting in my cupped hand, small and warm. Cautiously I let my fingers follow the sensual windings on its surface. During our first night together I was afraid of getting lost. Now I could make maps of your body, Daniel. One would show where all the scents are, another one would place all the different temperatures, yet another would reveal the spots my tongue, my lips find most attractive, and so on...

The church bell marks yet another short quarter.

* * *

Next morning when I wake up you are already gone, but you have left a note on my table and your scents in my bed.

I close my eyes, pull the blanket over my head and bury my face in my pillow. I've never been touched by anyone's essence the way I'm being touched by yours, Daniel. You are a whole temple of odors. I pretend to run around its pillars and along its passages, its smooth lines and structural vaults, its secret galleries and resting places, in search of strange and enchanting fragrances and flavors. Do you remember one of my first letters to you, where I likened you to an amusement park for my senses?

I ride my bike to the cliff. It's strangely autumnal and the small bay pretends to be an ocean, gray and dangerous, with long, sweeping waves. The reeds are bending wilder than ever as the wind playfully and often rather brutally grabs them for a moment, and then, just as suddenly, lets them go.

I take off my clothes, wedge them in a cleft to prevent their being blown away, and go down to the water. I miss you and I'm not really tiptoeing though I mainly use the front part of my feet. The wind is playing with the water. Drops are lifted from the gray waves to waft away. Of course I think of you as I dive and split the surface of the water. Eleven strokes later I am forced up to breathe. The water splashes over my head again and again. It is soft and warm and sad, as if knowing there will not be much more swimming this season. The water thrown up by the wind hits my face and makes me think of what I would like to do with you, what I know you would like to do with me.

There are a few men on the cliff, all more or less dressed. I'm the only one insisting that it's still summer. I'm the only one denying the cold. I conjure up your image. I think of your skin, which would have been goose-pimpled by now, and thus the process which had already started within me is even more intensified: a lust for touching, loving, whispering, penetrating...

I stay on the cliff for three hours, for three dives into the water. As I dress I now feel cold, at first unintentionally, then with a more conscious appreciation, as if I am welcoming the autumn, although I'm still a bit sad and doubtful. Never before have I experienced a summer like this. Never before have I been on a journey like this. What's next?

Eric and I made a long geographical journey our third year together. Among the countries we visited were Germany, Austria and Italy. We were in Florence for two days. I had a fever the whole time and don't remember much. I do of course remember Michelangelo's *David,* the one in marble at the museum, and the one in bronze looking down on the hazy city from a hill with a magnificent view but very few seats for a tired and feverish traveler. And I do remember, when we had descended to the houses and the streets, the dome of Santa Maria del Fiore suddenly looming over us as we passed an alley, and how something in its exterior, something that looked like an eye, watched us in an almost frightening way. And I remember looking out of the side window of a bus rumbling down a much too narrow street, seeing the terrified twisted face of a teenage girl the second before she and her bicycle were crushed between the bus and a projecting building. But she wasn't crushed. The bus driver or God or someone else quickly intervened, and the frightful moment was gone. But I still remember the girl's scream. All my other memories of Florence have been wiped out by the fever I had and the years that have passed. Eric didn't have a fever. He was sound and very present in Florence. He must have had a number of memories from our stay there. Do you still remember Florence, Eric? Are your memories, our memories, intact?

* * *

I search through one of Eric's photo albums until I find the pictures from Florence.

One of me was taken on a narrow, winding road leading up to the youth hostel. I'm standing in the middle of the road wearing denim shorts and a light blue T-shirt. No shoes. I hold a bottle of mineral water in one hand, a plastic bag in the other. Eric took the picture. I'm in it. But I don't remember.

I continue my search. And so I find a picture I do remember, a moment I can recall.

We reached the Gare de Lyon in Paris two days after we left Florence. My fever had vanished. I felt good, and happy.

We borrowed an apartment in Montmartre from some Swedish friends, and it became our Parisian base camp.

On the fourth day of our stay in the French capital we visited Centre Pompidou, the cultural center. It was warm, close to forty degrees Centigrade, although it was almost evening. Going up the escalators—enclosed in marvelous Plexiglas pipes that climbed the façade like some giant caterpillar—sickened us somewhat.

When we reached the top floor Eric talked ravishingly about the architecture. He stopped to look at some detail. I passed him and walked on toward the open terrace. I walked up to the metal fence and looked down on the old, slightly inclined square. The heat was not that palpable anymore; there was even a breeze up there. A few blocks away a church bell tolled seven times.

Then Eric called out my name. I turned and looked at him. The wind was softly blowing his hair about as he snapped the picture.

The rain pouring down in my backyard is strangely warm and there is a light smell of brimstone. We are waiting for the next clap of thunder. But, still, the only sound coming through my open window is of heavily falling rain, and almost drowned by that mighty sound are three tolls from my church's bell. It is late, almost midnight. A single, flickering candle on my sofa table is trying to subdue the dark. Its small flame lights up the orange petals of a gerbera nearby.

You are lying by my side, Daniel. It's the eighty-second day of our mutual journey and you tell me something about your mother, something about your family. You tell me of trips you have taken, places you have visited. You describe scents and environments, forms and patterns, and I travel with you as the rain keeps falling.

Earlier tonight you were sad. You talked of us—you and me and everybody—as temporary visitors in a room, a room in which we were born, in which we live and die, while the room itself stands untouched, unchanged. As if our selves—our lives, our experiences, our loves—mean nothing to this room. And so you were sad because it all seemed so paltry, while I tried—and still try—to make you, make us, look upon our limited time here as a challenge to experience something exciting and significant.

When the light has died and the rain has ceased I tell you about Eric. Afterward I lie listening to your breathing, Daniel, sharing your scents and the warmth of your body. Underneath my hand your heart is beating. Outside, the church bell tolls one.

"Sometimes when we're together I can feel Eric's presence, as if he's here," you say. "As if he is still around in some way. As if he wants to give us his approval, his support. Can you feel it too?"

And so we make love once again.

And so the journey continues.

Translated from Swedish by the author.

PROM KING

Rob Rosen

Ten years back, Jack was the prom king, Lisa his queen. Of course, he had other admirers, other queens, so to speak, eyeing him from afar (and a-close). Yours truly, to be exact. Though I was always more like the jester than royalty, skimming the edges of his court, catching stolen glances when he wasn't aware, bringing a smile to his face when he allowed my lowly, non-football-player presence.

Yes. Bitter, table for one. So sue me.

Anyway, he called me Chuckles, way back when. Though my name is Chuck. Didn't matter much, really; he could call me whatever he wanted to, just so long as he called. Day or night. Night especially. Of course, that, sadly, never happened.

Except that one time.

Mmm.

See, besides being the class clown, I was also something of a braniac. Straight-A student, debate team and chess club captain. Nerdy chic, I liked to call it. Not that anyone was all that eager to tack on the chic part, but still. In any case, I was surprised when he called and asked (begged) me to come over to help him study. Seems his football scholarship was hanging in the balance. He needed at least a C in biology in order to keep his grade point average where it needed to be.

Hence the call. The ask. The beg.

"I'll be right over," I eagerly replied, nearly breathless, and then quickly hung up. No way was I giving him the chance to change his mind.

"That was fast," he said, not ten minutes later. He was standing in his front door, wearing track shorts. Oh, and nothing else but a smile that shot a spark through my belly before ricocheting from one end of my body to the other.

"I, uh, I don't live that far away," I replied. Not that far if I drove eighty miles an hour, that is. Which I did. Red lights be damned.

His grin brightened, shaming the sun as it made its gradual descent that evening. "Cool," he said, showing me in, the door clicking behind me, causing my heart to skip a beat. And then suddenly I was in the lion's den. Well, the living room, really, but you get the picture. "Thanks again for coming over," he said, jumping on the couch, muscles flexing, belly taut, offering the faintest peek up his shorts before he got comfortable. Which made one of us.

"No problem," I said, trying (failing) to keep my voice from quivering. "I was studying for the same exam anyway." Sort of. I mean, I already had such a high grade that even if I bombed the exam, which was highly unlikely, I'd still probably get an A. In any case, I sat across from him and plopped my books down on a coffee table. It was then I noticed the silence. "Parents not home yet?"

He shrugged. "Late night at work. As usual. Just us, dude."

His sapphire-blue eyes bore into me, causing a swarm of butter-flies to flitter madly about in my gut. He scratched absentmind-edly at a dense pec, his index finger running through a smat-tering of curly blond chest hair.

I gulped and flicked open my textbook, willing myself to look away from him. See, I'd secretly been in love with Jack since the first grade. Head over heels. And now he was nearly naked and alone with me. Alone! I gulped again at the thought of it. Though perhaps this was the reward for my years of patience. And endless, albeit solo, jacking off to visions of him in my head. Amazingly, the visions couldn't even begin to compete with the reality. And there went that third gulp and the reason I had to look away. Mostly.

"What do you need help with, Jack?" I asked.

He sighed. "All of it," he replied, glumly. "Science just ain't my thing, Chuckles."

English didn't seem to be faring all that well, either. "Okay, let's just do the highlights then and hope for the best." My sigh echoed his, especially when he patted the seat next to him. The king was calling his dutiful subject to his side.

I paused, suddenly terrified, but joined him just the same. Not that my heart wasn't pounding a thousand beats a minute and my jeans weren't getting tight around the crotch. But the studying would be easier if we were next to each other, I reasoned. Plus, I could stare at him that way. Sideways, I mean. Eyes glued to the mound beneath the silk shorts. At the love-trail that meandered to his belly button. At his hairy thighs and boulder-dense calves.

Naturally, I gulped again.

Nonetheless, we really did study, my knee bumping his, my finger sliding against his hand as I pointed to something in his textbook, my shoulder pressed up tight to his shoulder. Seriously, it was enough to make a randy eighteen-year-old go over the edge. Where I precariously teetered for well over a couple of hours. Until we reached the chapter on anatomy.

He handed me a list of all the major body parts, external and internal. "Mister Peters said we'd need to know all of these. Their locations and their functions."

I scanned the list and quickly quizzed him. He failed like an alcoholic's liver. Like a smoker's lung. Like an impotent's willy. Meaning, Jack didn't know his ass from his elbow. Better still, Jack didn't know jack. "Did you miss that entire week of class, dude?" I asked, face tilted his way, those eyes of his again locked on mine.

"That was the week we made it to the state championships," he explained. "My mind was elsewhere." He grinned and shrugged. "Don't suppose a good game of Operation would help us, huh?"

Again I scanned the list. "Nope, no mention of a funny bone." I shrugged. "Go figure."

He stood, shorts bunching in all the right places. "Just show me then," he said. "Point and explain. On me."

I would've pinched myself, to see if this were one of my more vivid dreams, but it didn't seem prudent. Just in case it wasn't a dream. Which, of course, it wasn't. So I stood, willing my legs to hold me up. And my jean's zipper to hold up, too, because, man, was there ever some pressure building up.

And so we started, from his cranium on down, my fingers pointing, awkwardly touching and occasionally caressing one body part after the next. He alternately nodded and occasionally giggled, if I tickled him, as we went from one biological system to the next. From skeletal to muscular, circulatory to nervous (which I was, big time), respiratory to digestive, endocrine to lymphatic, and, lastly (gulp), reproductive.

My face blushed red as I stared at his midsection. "Yeah, um," I began. "If you were a female, we'd be talking about your ovaries, oviducts, uterus, vagina and, uh, mammary glands." I ran a finger across his pec; he shivered when I accidentally-on-purpose brushed his nipple.

He stared at me, suddenly nervous. Clearly, these were uncharted waters. "But I'm, uh, I'm not a female," he said, voice shaky. Talk about stating the obvious.

"Yeah, I know." I pointed to his groin, which seemed to have expanded as much as my lungs by that point. "Then, for you, there's the testes, seminal vesicles and the, uh, the *penis*." The last word barely escaped from between my rather parched lips.

And now he was blushing, a patch of crimson rising up his neck. "Um, *that* organ I already know about." He paused and slipped his finger inside the elastic waistband of his shorts. He stared down and in, and smiled.

Oh, to be so lucky. I thought to myself.

Except, then I was.

See, he paused, then looked up, my heart thumping as he again locked eyes with me. "Uh, one question on that though, Chuckles," he said, clearly thinking of just the right words to say. "I mean," he continued. "On the size."

"Size?" I asked. "What about it?"

His fingers were still inside the waistband, a hint of blond bush poking out. That gulp of mine made its triumphant reappearance as he continued. "I mean, what, uh, what's a *normal* size?"

I sat. My poor legs just couldn't take the strain anymore. "You, uh, you take showers with the team, Jack," I replied. "Don't you know?"

Again he paused. "They're all...they're all *soft* then."

"Oh," was about all I could manage, since my head was

about to explode. Both of them. The upper one and the lower one. "You mean, what's the normal size, uh, *hard*?"

He nodded. "I mean, I've only ever seen mine. And you can't tell on the Internet. Not really. And, well, I was just curious." All this he rolled out in a matter of about two seconds, though it seemed to land in slow motion inside my head. I mean, the guy I was furiously in lust with was talking with me about boner size. And his was a mere few inches away.

Still, I persevered. "I hear...I hear six inches is normal."

Again he nodded, quickly running from the room and just as quickly returning with, of all things, a ruler. "Six inches, huh?" And then he tried to stick said ruler inside his shorts. Which, of course, didn't work out so well. And then (gulp, gulp, and triple gulp), he said. "Here, you do it." And he handed me the ruler.

Well, he handed it and I promptly dropped it. Then I bent down, and when I looked back up, his shorts had dropped to the ground and his cock was jutting up and pointing just slightly to the left. I stifled a groan and, with trembling hands, slid the plastic ruler beneath his shaft. I looked back up at him. He was staring intently at me, a slight tic just above his eyebrow. "Seven and a half, Jack," I coughed.

He grinned. "Phew."

I stood back up and willed myself to keep my peepers off his pee pee. "Yeah, phew."

Only, he wasn't done with this line of questioning just yet. "What about you?" he asked.

Okay, so I glanced back down. Quickly. "What about me, what?"

He grabbed the ruler from my hand. "Your turn, Chuckles," he said. "Fair's fair. Unless you're scared, I mean. Of not being, well"—he pointed at his rather lengthy schlong—"you know."

Only, that's not what I was scared of. In any case, I figured, why tempt fate? So, slowly, I unzipped my jeans and then pushed them to my ankles. Needless to say, my prick was tenting my briefs something fierce. "Get the ruler ready," I coughed out, and then dropped my undies, until my cock was pointing at his and his at mine. Like two divining rods. Literally.

"Holy shit," he whispered.

I grinned. "It's eight inches, Jack," I told him. "No need for the ruler. Been there, done that." More than once, truth be told. Just to see if it was still growing.

He moved in, his pressed up snug against mine, a shock of adrenaline suddenly bursting through me like fireworks. "But mine is thicker," he made note.

I stared down, shocked that my dick was now butting up against his. That he was so close to me that I could smell his breath, smell the musk and sweat of him. "And your head is wider." I went for broke on that one, grabbing at it for effect. I mean, in for a penny, in for a pound, right?

His eyelids fluttered and a soft moan spilled out from between his lips. "That, uh, that feels good, Chuckles."

My hand moved further down, jacking at his impossibly stiff pole. "And that?"

The moan grew louder, deeper. "Better." He reached down and gave mine a tug and a stroke. "That okay?"

Gross understatement. "You get an A-plus for that one, Jack," I rasped.

He laughed and moved in closer, closer still. Then he leaned in. "I, uh, I have a secret to tell you, Chuckles," he whispered.

I craned my face up to his, both our hands working fast now, my balls bouncing as he stroked away. "What's that, Jack?" I replied, also in a throaty whisper.

And then, just as our lips were mere centimeters apart, the words about to fall from his mouth, two beams of light cast brightly through the living room window. "Fuck!" he hollered. "My parents are home." And, no, those weren't the words I'd been waiting for. Not even close. Not by a mile.

I nearly cried, but quickly got dressed instead, sadly stuffing my steely eight inches away, while Jack lifted up his shorts and hopped on the couch, a cushion covering himself up. I jumped over to the seat across from him and flipped open my biology book, just as the mister and missus walked inside.

Thankfully, they barely paid us any attention, because by then I could barely breathe and my entire body was twitching. And Jack looked even worse, beads of sweat trickling down his forehead.

"How's the studying going?" his mom asked, hanging up her jacket.

"Good," Jack blurted out. "Almost done. Chuck here was just about to leave."

"I was?" I asked, my heart breaking, shattering in a million pieces. "I mean, yes, I was." Jack wasn't even looking at me now, his face buried in his book, his body scrunched over the cushion, hiding his erection from them, from me. I stood and grabbed my stuff and headed for the door. "Good luck on the exam," I said, staring back his way, dying for his eyes to meet mine one last time. Even for a second.

They didn't. "Thanks," he said, with nothing but a wave my way.

I waited, but that was it. Then I left, the door once again clicking behind me. Except, now we were on opposite sides of it. No more Jack in nothing but his shorts and a radiant smile. No more sapphire eyes boring into me, squeezing my heart like a vise.

* * *

What we had done together that night was never spoken of. Finals came and went. He got a B in biology. Yippee for my tutoring skills. Then school ended and he went into his future and I went into mine. Separate.

But like I said, that was a long time ago. Ten years ago. Ten long years. Time for a high school reunion. Jack was there, of course. After all, the king can always come back and reclaim his throne, even a decade later. But, alas, my jester days were over. And so I watched from the sidelines, glad at least that he looked happy and healthy. If not downright handsome as all get out. Jack was all man now, the boy long vanished. Though the smile remained, causing those familiar butterflies of mine to take flight inside my belly.

And then he spotted me, eyes locked, the grin on his stunning face going into overdrive. And, oh, how my heart lit up at the sight of it. He waved and I waved back. Then he broke away, the court shocked at his sudden departure, especially when they realized where he was headed. To me, I mean.

"Hey, Chuckles," he said, his voice deeper than I remembered it, hand outstretched, flesh meeting flesh in an electric spark upon contact.

"Jack," I squeaked out. "You're, uh, you're looking well."

He nodded, that smile of his going full-on supernova. "You, too," he said, taking me in. "You, too." And then an awkward pause, his hand still in mine. "I, uh, I was hoping you'd be here."

I flushed, my legs suddenly going weak. "You were?"

He nodded. "I never got to say good-bye," he said, regret creeping into his voice.

"When school let out? After we graduated?" I asked. "Guess we were both just busy."

His nod turned to a shake. "No, not then." And I knew what he meant as he laughed and moved in closer, closer still. Then he leaned in. "I, uh, I still have that secret to tell you, Chuckles," he whispered.

I craned my face up to his, both our hands still gripped tightly together. "What's that, Jack?" I replied.

And then, just as our lips were mere centimeters apart, the words about to fall from his mouth, the words I'd been waiting ten years to hear now, two beams of light shot down from the stage "Fuck!" I muttered. "Not again!"

He was being called up there. Him and Lisa. The king and the queen. To start the first dance of the evening. He pulled his hand from mine, his smile turning for a split second into a frown. I watched as he made his way through the crowd, him coming from the right, Lisa from the left, then both ascending to the stage to take their rightful places. And, as good subjects, we all applauded and catcalled and whistled our approval. Because some things never change.

Or, maybe, sometimes they do.

The music started, a slow tune. The two of them looked at each other and then down at all of us, both of them walking back down the stairs and onto the dance floor. Only, Jack kept right on walking.

"You're joking, right?" I asked, my long-forgotten gulp returning as he again took my hand.

"Nah, Chuckles," he said, sweeping me up into his arms as the crowd gasped, a few claps emerging from different pockets. "Not anymore."

I rested my head on his shoulder as we began to dance. And then I pinched myself, just in case. "Not a dream," I whispered, with a sigh.

"Speak for yourself," he whispered back, twirling us around

the dance floor, the rest of the crowd soon pairing up and joining us.

Then I looked up and into his blue eyes twinkling beneath the disco ball's silver beams. "You were about to tell me something, if I recall correctly," I said, with a wink and a smile. "Twice now, in ten years."

He nodded and leaned in. "That secret," he said, his face radiant. "I, uh, I just wanted to tell you...ever since the first grade, I, well, I've had a secret crush on you."

No fucking way! I thought. "No fucking way!" I said.

"Way," he said, leaning in closer, our lips mere centimeters apart. And then not apart at all. It was a kiss worth a decade's wait. Heck, worth waiting since the first grade for. A kiss straight from a fairy tale, even. And the king and his jester danced and kissed their way into the night. And into their futures. Together.

And they lived, as they do in all great fairy tales, happily (gulp) ever after.

CODY BARTON

Martin Delacroix

Cody Barton tried killing himself, but he failed.

Then Cody came to live with us.

His dad dropped him off on our driveway. No hugs good-bye. Dr. Barton only waved from behind the wheel of his Audi before he drove away. This was days after Christmas. The afternoon was overcast and a damp breeze fluttered Cody's shoulder-length hair while he strode up our walkway.

I met Cody at the doorstep. The rope mark on his neck looked like a violet snake; it passed beneath his Adam's apple. Dark smudges appeared beneath Cody's eyes and a few zits dotted his cheeks. He carried a suitcase the size of a portable television in one hand, his skateboard in the other. A backpack hung from his shoulders.

"Are you all right?" was all I could think to say.

Cody wouldn't hold my gaze. He stared at his feet and shrugged.

"The Bartons' housekeeper found him hanging from a rafter

in their garage," my mom had told me the night before. "There was some sort of family argument beforehand."

Family argument? What's new?

Cody was my best friend; I'd known him since middle school. I had spent much time at his house and I knew his parents. Dr. Barton was okay: soft-spoken and reserved. But Cody's mom, Barbara, was a complete bitch. She hounded Cody about everything: his school grades, personal grooming, even his posture. Her voice was nasal and flavored with a Georgia drawl. I winced whenever I heard it.

When he was younger, Cody weathered his mom's insults silently. But once he reached high school, Cody started talking back. He'd argue with his mom in front of me. They would shout and sometimes throw stuff across the room. It made me so uncomfortable I avoided their home. Whenever Cody would ask me to visit him there, I'd suggest another meeting spot: my house, our neighborhood skatepark—anywhere but the Bartons'.

Finally, Cody stopped inviting me over altogether.

Weekends, he'd often spend Friday and Saturday nights with us, sleeping on an army cot in my bedroom. My parents didn't mind; they liked Cody, especially my mom. Cody and I would sit on the family room sofa—we'd play a video game or watch a movie—and Mom would enter with two glasses of iced tea. She'd run her fingers through Cody's rust-colored hair; sometimes she'd call him "sweetie" or "handsome." Cody would grin and his cheeks would redden.

"Your mom's the best," he'd tell me.

Now, Cody followed me into the house, his suitcase banging against his leg. In my room, the cot was already set up, equipped with sheets, a pillow and blanket. I pointed to a battered chest of drawers my dad had borrowed from a neighbor the day before.

"You can put your stuff in there," I said, "and there's room in the closet, too."

While Cody unpacked, I sat on my bed and watched. He placed his socks and underwear in the bureau's top drawer, his T-shirts, jeans and shorts in others. He tossed two pairs of athletic shoes into my closet, along with his skateboard. Then he draped a hooded sweatshirt and a jacket over clothes hangers.

The last thing Cody removed from his suitcase was a framed, five-by-seven photograph of Dean Barton, Cody's late brother. Dean had died the previous spring, victim of a hazing mishap at his University of Florida fraternity house. Just nineteen, he died of heatstroke while locked in the trunk of a car. The beer-sotted brothers who'd put Dean in the trunk forgot he was there, until it was too late.

I had known Dean before he left for college. He captained our high school's swim team, made National Honor Society, was elected to the homecoming court. Tall and blond, with a perpetual suntan and a mouthful of white teeth, Dean was the guy all of us aspired to be. Over three hundred people attended his memorial service.

After Dean's death, Cody changed: he talked less and rarely laughed. He avoided the few friends we had. Our passion, mine and Cody's, had always been skateboarding. In the past we'd spent countless hours grinding on the streets of Clearwater. But now Cody hardly skated at all. He smoked marijuana most every evening, spent hours alone in his bedroom listening to music or wandering the Internet on his laptop computer. His school grades worsened, and some days he actually smelled bad, like he hadn't showered or washed his hair for several days.

When I confronted him about these things, Cody only scowled.

He said, "Leave me alone, Zach."

So I did.

I waited for Cody to phone me, and sometimes I wouldn't hear from him for a week or more. He rarely slept at my house. The cot remained folded up in my closet, and I wondered if our friendship had reached an end.

Now, in my bedroom, Cody placed the photograph atop the bureau, next to his toothbrush and wallet. He stowed his suitcase in a corner, along with his backpack. The box springs wheezed when he sat next to me. Sunlight entered through a window above my headboard; it reflected in Cody's green eyes, highlighted freckles on his nose.

"Go on," he said, looking at me. "You can ask whatever you want; I don't care."

"Tell me why you did it."

He gazed into his lap. "I couldn't take her shit any longer."

"Your mom's?"

Cody nodded. He spoke in falsetto, mimicking his mother, complete with Georgia drawl. "'Dean made Honor Roll every term, why can't you? And why aren't you dating? Dean had a girlfriend his sophomore year.'"

Cody puckered one side of his face. "Why go on living with *her* in my life?"

I scratched my head, thinking, *I smell bullshit.*

Cody's explanation didn't ring true. I was pretty sure something else had driven Cody over the edge—exactly what I had no idea—but I didn't say anything.

According to my mom, Cody's therapist had insisted Cody *not* return to the Bartons' home after his brief stay in a psychiatric facility. Arrangements had been made between Cody's folks and mine. Cody would live under our roof, at least until the school year's end, when Cody and I would graduate. Each month the Bartons would write my parents a check for Cody's food and incidentals.

Now, in the bedroom, I looked at Cody and wondered what thoughts dwelled inside his head. Was he angry his suicide attempt had failed? And how did he feel about living with my family?

Cody glanced at his wristwatch. He rose and plucked a bottle of prescription pills from his backpack. Placing one tablet on his tongue, he swallowed.

"What's that?" I asked.

"Antidepression medication."

When I made a face, Cody raised his shoulders and puffed out his cheeks.

"Sorry, Zach; I guess I'm kind of crazy."

The day we returned to school, a band of thunderstorms spread across central Florida. Charcoal-colored clouds filled the morning sky. Raindrops stippled the surface of mud puddles. Cody and I sat in my car at a stoplight, both of us dressed the same: beanie caps, faded T-shirts, jeans and skateboard shoes. Our backpacks rested on the rear seat.

Cody's T-shirt did not conceal his rope marks. My mom had offered Cody a tube of cosmetic cover up, but he declined it. "Everyone knows," he told her. "Why try to hide it?"

Our school had its fair share of assholes, guys who reveled in making other people miserable. I wondered what might happen during the hours ahead. How would people react to Cody? To *me* when they saw us together?

Cody stared out the windshield at passing traffic. His voice quivered when he spoke.

"Will you walk to first period class with me? I don't think I can do it alone."

"Sure," I said. "No problem."

In the school parking lot, a few people pointed and stared. One jerk grabbed his throat; he made loud, strangling noises and his antics caused other people to laugh. Cody and I pretended not to notice. We entered our monolithic, two-storied school through glass doors. Inside, a crush of voices echoed in the hallways. More people pointed at Cody; at me too. They stared and whispered. My pulse raced and the tops of my ears burned. I kept my gaze straight ahead, avoiding eye contact altogether.

Just get Cody to class…

Things went okay until we reached Cody's locker. Someone had fashioned a full-size noose from a length of cotton clothesline; it hung from the finger hole in Cody's locker door handle. Cody's face turned ashen when he saw the noose. Down the hall, two guys cackled.

"Ignore them," I whispered.

A tear trickled from one corner of Cody's eye.

"I *hate* this fucking place," he said.

On a Thursday afternoon, I drove Cody to an after-school appointment with his therapist. The therapist's office wasn't far from Oleander Park, a green space fronting Tampa Bay. After dropping Cody off, I drove straight to the park.

I'd visited Oleander two dozen times at least, and I'd always sit on a particular bench in an isolated spot. Then I'd wait for something I sorely needed: sex.

The park was a notorious cruise area for gay men; I'd learned this through articles published in the local newspaper. I'd go there after school, when my folks were at work and my whereabouts wouldn't be questioned. I met guys at Oleander who would never patronize a gay club, attractive but closeted men, some of them married.

I was queer, no question about it. I craved the feel of a man's muscles, the weight of his cock on my tongue and the taste of his semen. For some guys my age masturbation was enough, I guess. But not me; I needed another man's flesh.

Of course, nobody knew about my visits to Oleander. I'd have died of embarrassment if they had. I considered gay sex sordid and nasty, but still I craved it like some folks needed illegal drugs. Too young at eighteen to visit gay bars, I satisfied my urges at the park. I didn't feel good about myself after these encounters, but my guilt didn't keep me from frequenting Oleander.

This particular Thursday, a warm breeze blew and the sun shone, casting shadows of slash pines onto the park's sandy soil. I strode down a sidewalk, hands in my pockets, till I reached my bench. Shrubbery surrounded me on three sides and pine needles carpeted the ground. Few people were about. I crossed a knee with an ankle, sucked my cheeks and gazed at a squirrel hopping about the limbs of a turkey oak. Checking my wristwatch, I saw ten minutes had passed since I'd left Cody at the therapist's. At best I had a half hour to kill.

I squirmed on the bench, glancing here and there. Would I fail to meet someone this visit? Would I leave dissatisfied?

Be patient; give it time.

Minutes later someone cleared his throat. I glanced toward a clump of saw palmettos. A man stood among the bushes, a decent-looking guy with dark hair and eyes, probably in his late twenties. I'd never seen him in Oleander Park before. When my gaze met his, he grinned at me and crooked a finger.

Go on, get moving.

Up close, the guy looked even better: a bit of stubble on his cheeks and chin, muscles bulging under his T-shirt, another bulge in his blue jeans. I followed him to a clearing where passersby wouldn't see us. Used condoms and damp wipes littered the ground.

He turned on his heel to face me. "I'm Todd," he whispered.

"I'm Zach."

"You're cute, Zach. Do you suck cock?"

I nodded. Already, my pulse raced. I salivated like a starving man invited to a feast.

Todd tapped his zipper with a fingertip. "I have eight inches. Want a taste?"

Eight inches? Fuck, yeah...

I sank to my knees. Hands trembling, I reached for the button at the waist of Todd's jeans and popped it open. I couldn't wait to get my mouth on Todd's cock. While I lowered his zipper, he reached into his back pocket. I figured he wanted to play safe; I assumed he'd offer me a condom, but I was wrong.

Boy, was I wrong.

Todd flashed a badge in my face instead.

"You're under arrest, Zach."

An explosion went off inside my head. *He's a cop, stupid; you're screwed.*

Then I thought, *What will Mom and Dad say?*

Oh, shit...

The ride to County Jail was awful. Todd and another officer sat in the cruiser's front seat, discussing banalities, while I sat in back with my hands cuffed before me, listening to their radio bark. I'd never felt more scared or humiliated in my life. I stared out my window, shaking like a sapling in a storm. Tears rolled down my cheeks. How could I have been so careless?

Things worsened when we reached the jail. The intake officer was someone I knew. Her son had performed in a school play with me and we'd rehearsed at their house a few times. She had seemed nice back then, but now she arched an eyebrow and scowled.

"Zach, what are *you* doing here?"

I lowered my gaze while my cheeks flamed.

I spent three hours sitting in a windowless cell, along with a couple of tattooed street thugs and a pale, skinny guy hallucinating on LSD. The skinny guy wouldn't stop babbling nonsense. We all wore orange jumpsuits and slip-on sneakers. I felt lower than pond scum. The cell stank of ammonia and human sweat. Above us, a fluorescent ceiling fixture hummed and flickered. I sat on a bench, staring at the concrete floor while my stomach churned. The enormity of my arrest had settled over me like a leaden blanket.

You're fucked, I kept telling myself, *totally fucked.*

My dad posted bail for me. After I changed into street clothes, I met him in the jail's reception area. He stood there with his hands in his pockets, staring at the floor with his shoulders hunched.

"Dad?"

He lifted his chin and his gaze met mine. I trembled like a kid in a spook house, feeling fear, disgust and shame. Why had this happened to me? Would my parents hate me for what I'd done?

Dad didn't say anything. He took me by a forearm, guided me through the exit doors and into the parking lot. The sun was down and stars appeared in the night sky. Crickets chirped among the trees. Standing next to our car, I fell apart and wept like a four-year-old.

"Daddy, I'm so sorry."

He took me in his arms and held me close.

"It's okay, son. It'll be all right."

* * *

The night of my arrest, my parents didn't lecture me. When Dad and I got home, my mom hugged me and asked if I was okay.

"I guess," I said. "Can you forgive me?"

"We love you, Zach; this doesn't change a thing. Go take a shower."

I felt filthy from my stay at the jail. Warm water raining on my skin soothed me and helped me feel human again. But I couldn't get memories from jail out of my head: the stink, the creepy prisoners, and the sordidness of it all.

Afterward, Cody and I sat in my bedroom with the door closed. I told him everything: how many times I'd visited Oleander Park, the sex acts I'd performed there, how I'd known I was gay since I was twelve, and how badly I craved intimacies with men. The words poured out of me like water from a spigot. I guess I'd always wanted to share my secrets with someone, and now I could.

Cody listened without comment. When I'd finished talking, he tapped his chin with his fingertips. "I don't understand something," he said.

"What's that?"

"How come you didn't tell me these things before? I thought we were best friends."

"We *are*," I said, "but sucking cock's not something I'm proud of. I wasn't sure how you'd react if I told you I was queer."

Cody made a face. "That's how little you trust me?"

His remark got me angry. I spoke without thinking first. "You're a fine one to talk: you've lived here three weeks but you still haven't explained."

"Explained what?"

"The reason you tried killing yourself. And don't give me that crap about your mom. It was something else, I know."

Cody looked away and rubbed his lips together.

"Come on," I said, "tell me."

Cody went to the cot, climbed under the covers and turned away from me.

Most everyone at school used Internet social networking, so it didn't take long for news of my arrest to spread. Altered photos of me appeared online: I'd have a cock in my mouth or a dildo up my ass. I received dozens of insulting emails, a couple of threats too. In the school parking lot, someone spray-painted FAGGOT on my car.

I was shoved and kicked numerous times in our school's hallways. Guys called me every name in the book: *fairy, fudge-packer, sissy boy, pervert* and *cocksucker*, to name a few. They made kissing sounds behind my back. People I'd *thought* were my friends ceased talking to me altogether. Suddenly I was a leper.

The only person who stuck with me was Cody. We'd walk to first period together each morning, eat lunch together in the cafeteria. Each afternoon we'd walk to my car together. None of this was easy for Cody, I'm sure. Guys called Cody and me "asshole buddies"; they accused Cody—right to his face—of being my boyfriend. But none of it dissuaded Cody from standing with me.

"If someone tries to beat you up," he said, "they'll have to fight me too."

After a couple of weeks, guys grew tired of harassing me. The insults tapered off and people stopped staring. My arrest became yesterday's news. But my former "friends" still avoided me. My cell phone rarely chimed and my text message inbox remained empty. Socially, I was a complete pariah. I went through my school days speaking to no one but my teachers and Cody.

Thank god for Cody.

Since moving to our house, he'd become more like his old self. He had emptied his bag of marijuana down the garbage disposal. He took more pride in his appearance, put more effort into school. Each afternoon, we'd study in my room. In our free time we played video games, rode our skateboards and watched TV. Or we drove around town in my car, not talking much, just cruising the streets.

Our misfortunes had brought us closer together, I think. We'd both been shamed before our peers and socially ostracized. Lesser boys might've gone crazy—maybe even jumped off a bridge—but together we managed to survive. On campus we kept our grades up, our chins as well.

"Fuck people at school," Cody said. "Who needs them?"

You're right, I thought.

All I need is your friendship.

I woke to the sound of Cody's whimpering. I'm a fairly sound sleeper, but he made plenty of noise. He lay in fetal position, under the blanket on his cot. I glanced at my nightstand clock; the time was three a.m. Cody's knees chugged; his feet kept thrusting from beneath his covers. Silvery moonlight poured into the room through a pair of double-hung windows. I knelt beside Cody and shook his shoulder. When Cody didn't respond, I poked his ribs.

"Wake up."

He turned toward me and his eyes fluttered open.

"What is it?"

"I think you're having a bad dream."

He flipped onto his back and didn't say anything.

"What were you dreaming about?"

"The same shit as always."

"What?"

Cody looked at me. Then he returned his gaze to the ceiling.

"Tell me," I said. "I'm staying right here 'til you do."

He drew a breath, released it. "I dreamt about my brother."

"Dean?"

Cody nodded. "In the dream I stood next to the car he died in. I heard him kick the trunk lid and holler for help. He knew I was there; he even called my name. My parents watched. They shouted at me to do something but I didn't have a key to the trunk. It was...awful."

"Have you dreamt this before?"

"Many times, Zach."

Jesus, I thought. *Poor Cody...*

Spring break arrived in late March. Cody and I had performed well in school, so my folks agreed to rent us a room at the beach for three nights.

"I'm trusting you," my mother said. "No drunken parties."

And I thought, *Parties require friends, Mom. We don't have any, remember?*

But I only nodded.

The motel manager puffed on a cigarette while he checked us in. Students from assorted high schools and colleges occupied most of the rooms. Kids were all over the place, on the pool deck and in corridors. Boys guzzled beer, girls sipped wine coolers. The scent of burning marijuana was pervasive.

Our first night there, while swimming in the motel pool, we met a couple of guys from University of Florida. Ten minutes into the conversation, one guy told us the name of his fraternity and Cody's face turned white as an egg. He glanced at me and shook his head, very subtly. I cleared my throat. Changing the subject, I asked the UF guys if they might buy us beer, since

Cody and I were underage.

An hour later, Cody and I sat in our room on our lumpy beds while a case of Budweiser chilled in our mini-fridge. We sipped from cans, both of us wearing only board shorts, while Cody spoke of the boys from UF.

"I can't believe it. Of all the guys we had to meet..."

"Look," I said, "they don't know you're Dean's brother."

"True, but still it's weird. They could be the ones who—"

"Let's talk about something else."

While we gabbed, I studied Cody's physique. Like me, he was skinny and pale, with a smooth chest and a narrow waist. Copper-colored fuzz dusted his calves. In one leg of his shorts, his cock bulged and the sight of it made me hunger for sex.

By midnight we had killed most of the beer. We lay on our respective beds, listening to reggae music on my portable player. I didn't drink alcohol too often—neither did Cody—and both of us slurred our words. When I rose to visit the bathroom, I staggered and nearly fell. I stood before the toilet, swaying. Half my urine ended up on the floor. I didn't even bother flushing or zipping up, I just stumbled out of the bathroom with my cock hanging out of my board shorts. Then I fell backward onto my bed.

Cody looked at me and rolled his eyes. "You're shit-faced, you know. You forgot to put your dick away."

The alcohol emboldened me, made me feel reckless. I looked down at my groin, then at Cody.

"Why don't *you* put it away for me?"

Cody made a face and snickered. "Are you making a pass at me?"

"Maybe," I said. "I'm so horny I could fuck a goat."

Cody made a bleating sound. "You sure know how to flatter a guy."

I jabbed at my mattress with a fingertip. "How about it?"

Cody drew a deep breath. He swung his feet to the carpet and placed his hands on his knees while my pulse pounded in my head. This was uncharted territory for me and Cody. We were best friends, sure. But what would he say?

Cody licked his lips. He looked at the door, then at me.

"Tell you what, Zach: I'll sleep in your bed and we can do whatever you'd like. Just don't tell anyone, okay?"

Holy crap…

My cock stiffened—it looked like a runaway banana—but I felt a tinge of guilt. Would I regret this once I sobered up? Was I taking advantage of Cody?

"Look," I said, "you don't have to do this."

Cody put his hands on his hips and a little smile played on his face.

"I *want* to, Zach. I really do."

Cody locked the deadbolt, engaged the door's security chain. He went to the bathroom and used the toilet. After flushing, he switched off the lights. Our drapes were thin. Glow from the motel's corridor lights entered the room, enough so I could see.

Cody stood beside my bed. Looking down at me, he loosened his shorts' drawstring and let them drop. I'd never seen Cody's cock before. It was long and pale, with a head shaped like a strawberry. His pubic bush was copper colored.

"Hey," Cody said.

I looked up into his face.

"How come I'm the only naked guy here?"

Chuckling, I shoved my board shorts down my legs and kicked them away. Then I scooted over, making room for Cody. The bedsprings sighed when he lay beside me. His skin and hair smelled like pool chlorine. I lay on my back and Cody placed his cheek on my chest. He draped an arm across my waist, brought a knee to mine. His leg fuzz tickled my leg fuzz while he seized my erection in his fingers. He worked my foreskin back and forth. Then, shifting position, he took half my cock into his mouth and sucked it like a regular at Oleander Park.

I crinkled my forehead, thinking, *Huh?*

We were both drunk, of course. But something didn't feel quite right. I told myself, *This is* far *too easy.*

"Cody?"

He let my cock slip from his mouth. "What?"

"Have you done this before?"

He chuckled. "Lots of times."

"With who?" I said.

"You *don't* want to know."

"Of course I do."

"Are you sure?"

"Yeah, go ahead and tell me."

Cody let out his breath.

"Zach, I was my brother's lover for the longest time."

Huh? Dean and Cody?

I felt like someone had punched me in the stomach. My vision blurred and a flash went off inside my head. My cock went limp as a dishrag. I pushed Cody away, sat up straight and flicked on the nightstand lamp. Cody's lips shone with spit. Both of us squinted in the brightness while our chests heaved.

"I don't believe this," I said. "How come you never told me?"

He raised a shoulder. "How come *you* never told me about Oleander Park?"

I fell onto my back and studied the popcorn ceiling, while questions flooded my brain. How long had Cody's affair with Dean lasted? What kind of sex acts had they performed and how often? Was Cody gay like me? Had he enjoyed lovemaking with his brother? Or had he simply submitted to Dean's will? Dean had dated girls in high school, real beauties. Had it all been a cover?

I didn't ask Cody about these things; they could wait.

I had something more important on my mind.

"As long as we're getting secrets out of the way..."

"What?"

"Tell me why you tried killing yourself? I want the truth this time."

Cody dropped his gaze and nodded.

"Turn off the light," he said. "Then I'll tell you."

Details of Cody relationship with his brother weren't all that complicated. When Cody had been fourteen, and Dean a year older, they'd experimented sexually while the Bartons vacationed in the Bahamas. The boys started with mutual masturbation, advanced to oral sex, then anal.

"Dean was great in bed," Cody told me. "He'd done it with guys before."

Both brothers felt enthralled by their intimacies. They made a pact before returning to Florida: they'd become lovers, but no one, *nobody,* must know.

"Dean said if anyone found out, he'd have disaster on his hands. His reputation at school was important, he said. He had definite plans for his future: college, law school, and politics."

I lay there in darkness with Cody's head resting on my sternum. I didn't say a word.

"It was crazy," Cody said. "I'd pass Dean in the school hallway and he'd be talking with some girl he dated. He'd give me a wink and then I'd ask myself, 'What would the girl say if she knew?' Or I'd overhear Dean talking on the phone with his swim team buddies. He'd mention fucking this girl or that one, and I'd recall him fucking *me* the night before."

I rubbed the tip of my nose. "Did you love Dean?"

"Of course I did. When he left for college, I thought I'd lose my mind. I kept calling him during fall semester—to see if I could come up to Gainesville for a visit—but he always said no 'cause he had no privacy there.

"Dean told me, 'Wait for Thanksgiving, little brother. I'll come home and we'll be together.'"

I twirled a lock of Cody's hair around my finger.

"Of course," Cody said, "Dean never made it home. When he suffocated in that car trunk, I grew so depressed *I* wanted to die. Why go on living if I didn't have Dean in my life? I bought a length of rope, learned how to tie a noose from the Internet. It took me many months to work up the courage, but I finally did it. I figured death would bring me peace."

I shuddered, thinking of Cody hanging in his garage. "My mom told me there was an argument at your house, just before—"

"We had a blowup all right, on Christmas Day, at the dinner table. My mom said it wasn't the same without Dean during the holidays, how we'd never understand the loss she 'felt in her heart.'

"It made me want to puke. I thought of the last time I'd made love with Dean, the night before he left for Gainesville. I told my mom, 'You didn't even *know* Dean. I was closer to him than you or Dad or anyone else. I'm the one who's suffering here.'

"My mom said something like, 'If you loved Dean you wouldn't have disappointed him so often. You never lettered in a sport; you never dated girls, were never popular like Dean. He felt embarrassed by you and your slouchy friends.'

"When she said that, I...*exploded*. I stood up and threw a gravy boat across the room; it hit the wall and shattered. I said, 'Dean wasn't just my brother, Mom; he was my boyfriend. Do you hear me? He was my *lover*.'"

"Holy shit, Cody."

He chuckled deep in his throat. "Yeah: holy shit. At that point, the toothpaste was out of the tube. I'd disappointed my parents before, of course. But now they knew about me and Dean. They'd hate me forever, I knew, 'cause I'd destroyed their vision of who Dean was."

Cody rearranged his limbs and cleared his throat.

"I had no one left to love me, Zach. It was time to die."

We lay there in silence for a bit, just breathing and thinking. I tried to imagine how lonely Cody must've felt Christmas Day and how badly he must've missed his brother.

Cody turned his head and looked at me.

"Any more questions?"

I shook my head.

Cody and I didn't have sex at the beach motel. His revelation about his brother had shocked me so badly I couldn't *think* of touching Cody. I kept seeing visions of Cody and Dean in my head, the two of them surreptitiously making love while the rest of us remained clueless. I felt foolish, like the last guy in the room who's let in on the joke.

I imagined how Cody's parents must've felt when Cody thrust reality into their faces.

No wonder Cody couldn't return home.

During the remainder of our motel stay, Cody and I busied ourselves with walks on the beach, dining at fast-food joints, and sunning ourselves by the pool. We bought a bottle of Canadian whiskey, courtesy of the UF boys, and our last two nights we drank the stuff mixed with ginger ale until we both passed out. We didn't discuss Dean or sex or anything remotely personal again.

I wasn't ready to.

* * *

Spring break ended. We returned to school and our empty social life. Cody slept in his cot, I in my bed. We'd both been accepted to University of Central Florida, but attending there wasn't an option for Cody. At the dinner table one night, he said his parents had refused to pay for his education.

"I'm on my own after high school," he told me and my folks. "I'll find a job, attend community college part-time. It'll be okay."

My mom looked like she would cry. She told Cody, "You'll always have a home with us."

My dad nodded in agreement.

I signed up for fall semester at UCF. My folks sent them a deposit check. Then, during the last week of May, Cody and I walked across the school's auditorium stage, looking ridiculous in our disposable caps and gowns. We both shook hands with the principal while my folks smiled and applauded. My dad took photos with his digital camera.

Cody's parents did not attend.

In mid-August, Cody's mom died unexpectedly, from an "aortic aneurysm." A blood vessel near her heart burst. In the space of ten minutes, she bled to death at the Bartons' country club, after collapsing on the putting green. Her obituary described her as a "loving wife and mother." When Cody saw it in the newspaper, he shook his head.

"Bullshit," was all he had to say.

I went to the funeral only because I felt I should be there for Cody. We both wore starched shirts, neckties and khaki pants. The day was overcast, with a smell of rain in the air. At the Bartons' family plot, a breeze ruffled Cody's hair while they lowered his mom's casket into the ground. Cody, I noticed, wasn't observing the goings-on. Instead, he kept his gaze on Dean's headstone.

That night, lightning flashed outside my bedroom window. Thunder rumbled so hard the house shook. Cody's cot frame creaked.

"Zach, are you still awake?"

"Yeah, this storm's keeping me up."

"Me too; I can't sleep."

We decided to play cards. I flicked on my nightstand lamp and Cody joined me on my bed. We sat facing each other, legs crossed at our shins, both wearing boxer shorts. I shuffled the deck and dealt. Then we played gin rummy, arranging our tricks on the blanket and saying little.

All summer long, Cody and I had power-raked people's Bahia lawns for cash. It was hard, sweaty work but paid well. In ten weeks we'd earned more than we could have bagging groceries an entire year. We were both tanned and fit, but skinny as ever. The muscles in my back and arms ached from the day's labors and I shifted my weight on the mattress, trying to get comfortable.

In a week, we'd return the power rake to the rental place. Then my dad would drive me to Orlando with my belongings and my college days would commence.

"Promise you won't pledge a fraternity," my mom had begged me.

I promised. What fraternity would pledge a guy with toothpick limbs and hair past his shoulders?

Now, in my room, Cody drew from the deck. "I'll miss you when you go," he said.

I nodded. How would it feel, not waking next to Cody each morning?

I told him, "At least you won't have to sleep on the cot. You'll like this bed."

After discarding, Cody looked up. "Will you do something for me, before you leave?"

I asked what.

He placed a hand on my knee and squeezed.

My eyebrows gathered. I looked at Cody's hand, then his face.

"Just once," he said. "It's been a rough day and I don't want to sleep alone."

I didn't know what to do. I thought of Dean's perfection. He'd been *way* out of my league; there was no way I could measure up to him and what he'd meant to Cody.

Say something.

"I'm not your brother," I told Cody. "I'm just a skater with zits."

Cody reached for my cheek and stroked it with his thumb. "It doesn't matter, Zach. You're my best friend; my *only* friend."

I hadn't touched a man sexually since my arrest. Already my cock was stiff and my pulse quickened.

Do it, stupid; do it for Cody.

Do it for you, too.

We lay naked on my bedsheets, Cody and I, each guy gripping the other's erection. Our lips smacked and our tongues rubbed. My heart thumped while my belly did flip-flops. I kept running my fingers through Cody's hair, marveling at its thickness and texture. I kissed his eyelids, his forehead and the tip of his freckled nose. When he took my cock in his mouth and sucked the glans, I groaned so loud I'm surprised my parents didn't hear me.

Actually, I think they did.

Cody worked my cock with his tongue and lips. It felt heavenly. His mouth was warm and wet, so sensual. I shifted position so I could return the favor. Then we both slurped away. I loved the scent of Cody's crotch. How *different* this was from sex in Oleander Park. I was making love with my best friend, the guy who'd stood by me when no one else would.

What a fool I'd been, turning down Cody at the beach motel. Sure, I'd been angry because he'd hidden his sex life from me all those years, but hadn't *I* done the same to Cody? Now that he was in my bed, I couldn't get enough of him. I wrapped my arms around his waist and squeezed as hard as I could.

Okay, I wasn't Dean Barton—I didn't have his looks or his athleticism—but at least I was there for Cody. I found Cody's lanky frame sexy; I liked touching him intimately. Maybe I could offer him a small measure of what he needed. Not just tonight, but in the future, if he'd let me.

UCF's only a ninety-minute drive from Clearwater. Maybe—

"Zach?"

"Yeah?"

"Will you fuck me?"

I greased my cock with lube from the nightstand drawer. Then I greased Cody's. He straddled me and sat on my erection. It was like nothing I'd ever experienced. I felt the clench of his pucker, the warmth of his gut when I entered him. Moonlight let me see the expressions on Cody's face while I thrust inside his body and he stroked himself. He looked drugged, as though he were far removed from reality.

A shiver ran through me when I came. My lungs pumped and my body jerked each time I shot. I closed my eyes while fireworks exploded in my head. Moments later, Cody cried out my name when he blew his load. His semen sprayed my chest and collarbone; it felt warm and viscous, teeming with his life force.

My cock still inside him, Cody bent at the waist and kissed my eyebrows. "That was wonderful, Zach. Is it okay if I tell you I love you?"

Tears leaked from the corners of my eyes. Snot crowded my nose and my lips quivered. I felt completely overwhelmed.

This is all you've ever needed: Cody's love. Screw Oleander Park and screw the kids who bullied us at school. Screw Cody's parents, too. They never deserved him, but I do.

I've earned Cody's love by being his friend.

My mother called to me from beyond the bedroom door.

"Zach, are you and Cody okay?"

I wiped my eyes and sniffled. Then I cleared my throat.

"Yeah, Mom," I said.

"We're both fine."

HELLO, YOUNG LOVERS

Simon Sheppard

Can anyone—anyone—dance around wearing a harness and well-filled codpiece *nearly* as well as Jake Shears?

Shears's band, Scissor Sisters, is onstage, and Buster, though at work, is loving every ultraqueer, retro-disco moment of it. It's not a bad job, really. He's been employed at the venue for well over a decade and a half, since some of tonight's audience was prepubescent. Since before a few of them were born. Now he's shockingly middle-aged, but not too old to rock and roll. Nor too old to appreciate a handsome, nearly naked hunk singing about taking your mama out all night, while prancing around a stage just forty feet away.

The audience is, of course, wildly into the band, too. Packed like sardines into the pit—the area just below the front of the stage—they jump, shimmy and all but dry-hump one another while Buster, perched at the top of the staircase to the pit, looks down and smilingly surveys the scene. Lots of cute guys, some of them already shirtless, plenty of them bears, others hairless and thin. If many of the shows he works at—metal, thrash metal, death metal, whatever—attract a near-unanimous crowd of hets, the Sisters' fans are flagrantly, gloriously non-straight.

Buster is enjoying himself. Thoroughly. He wishes that Charlie were with him. Not that Charlie would have enjoyed the show; dance music was hardly his thing. Beethoven and Vaughn Williams, more likely, and maybe some ambient electronica when he'd wanted background music to do his work to. It was one of the things he and Charlie had disagreed on, even when they were living together, even when they were desperately in love.

Buster had first met Charlie one morning in the park. It hadn't really been love at first sight, more like lust. "Cute dog," Charlie had said. Caesar was often a conversation starter, worth his weight in Milk-Bones.

"Thanks. What're you doing?" As though the binoculars around the stranger's neck and the field guide in his hand weren't clues enough.

"Birding," the good-looking man said. "There's a tree full of cedar waxwings just over there." He pointed, but Buster kept looking at the man's face, not at the tree. He was out cruising for hum jobs, not hummingbirds.

"Am I too nerdy for you, y'think?" The handsome guy smiled, shatteringly.

"Nah," Buster said.

And that had been pretty much it. Within an hour they were in bed together, within a month they were sharing an apartment. Buster had never believed in love, not really, but there they were, sharing an immoderate amount of happiness.

After several failed relationships—one of which had crashed and burned quite spectacularly—Buster had become pretty cynical about the possibility of Happiness Ever After. Charlie changed that. Love, Buster finally figured out, was not some great, overwhelming object, but rather a succession of shared moments. At first it was things as simple as making waffles from scratch together every Sunday morning. But as their lives became more and more entwined, they came to share one another's interests. Charlie taught Buster about birding, and though it initially made him feel like a geek, he soon could distinguish between a Brewer's blackbird and a boat-tailed grackle. For his part, Buster persuaded his lover to overcome his fears and learn to scuba dive; it wasn't long till handsome Charlie was putting on his buoyancy control device and descending to seventy feet.

And then there was cruising...the boat kind, not the sex kind. It was something neither had been interested in, not till their friends Henry and Ian sold them on the idea. But they came to love it. When, following a day of diving on Grand Turk, Buster and Charlie had stood on the aft of the promenade deck, watching the sun set over the wake, the world had never seemed so achingly beautiful. And then they went back to their cabin, where Charlie gave Buster the greatest blow job of his life.

It's not that they became identical twins, not quite. Buster never grasped Charlie's enthusiasm for the astringencies of twelve-tone music. Charlie, for his part, had no love for Nick Cave or the Velvet Underground, and he damned as "pap" Buster's favorite dance-pop guilty pleasures: the Pet Shop Boys, and even more shamefully, Erasure. Mid-period Madonna. And Gaga, of course. (Sure, they did, good homosexuals both, share a love of show tunes, but Buster gravitated toward the *schmaltz* of Rogers and Hammerstein, while Charlie preferred the more cerebral Sondheim.)

Still, schisms in musical taste didn't prevent them from

spending year after year together. Even when Charlie's trips to the park became more about cruising than birding, even after Buster started going to dance bars to pick up men, their mutual affection and respect remained firm, only grew.

Somewhere along the line, Charlie's very wealthy father passed away, and Charlie no longer had to work; he approached his very early retirement with alacrity and joy. Buster, though, decided to keep his job, despite Charlie's offer to support him. He cherished his self-sufficiency, and besides, he liked teaching. Loved it, really. And there was his part-time gig at the rock venue, too, a job he'd held since the days when Jerry Garcia was alive and almost well. When Charlie spotted a too-good-to-pass-up bargain flight to Cozumel, Buster encouraged him to take a break while he, Buster, was busy grading midterms, and go do some diving at Palancar Reef. In a way, Buster was semi-guiltily happy to have the place to himself for a while.

"Bye, sweetie. Don't work too hard."

"No worries. Say hi to the fishies for me."

"See you soon."

Buster was listening to Radiohead—he remembered that vividly—when the call came through. There'd been an accident. And though Charlie's dive buddy had done his best, that was that. Charlie was gone.

Gone.

And it was, Buster couldn't help but feeling, his fault.

Scissor Sisters have just finished up a song Buster has never heard before. Maybe it's from their new album. "You've really got to keep these stairs clear," he says to a couple of teenage girls. They move, reluctantly.

Ana Matronic launches into "Tits On the Radio" while bandmate Shears, singing backup, cavorts, half-dressed, beside her. Buster scans the gyrating mass of flesh in the pit.

And that's when Buster sees The Boy.

It's not the first time he's noticed him. Earlier, during the walk-in, before the forgettable opening band had taken the stage, The Boy, making his way into the pit, had headed down the stairway Buster had been assigned to. Before The Boy got down the stairs, though, he had turned to Buster and said, "Nice glasses."

"Thanks." Buster prided himself on his choice in eyewear. And on his taste in young men; this one was fairly astonishing, a bit geeky, unbelievably cute, with a little goatee and a big smile, wearing glasses himself, albeit nondescript wire-rims. Buster could easily imagine The Boy's body: skinny, smooth, quite unlike Charlie's hairy, chunky form, and all the more desirable for that. He idly hoped The Boy's dick was on the small side; Buster liked to be the well-hung one.

Not that the skinny kid was in any real way a sexual prospect. He liked Buster's glasses, he was being friendly. There were guys The Boy's age who liked older men, true; Buster had ended up in bed with more than a few of them. But it was stupid, he knew, to get his hopes up, especially while he was on duty. A sexual-harassment complaint was the last thing he needed...not that the kid would have lodged one, but still...

And Buster hated humiliation.

After a shared smile, The Boy descended into the pit and made his way toward the other side, to be lost in the mass of heaving flesh when the lights went down.

During intermission, though, they crossed paths again. The Boy descended Buster's stairs again, this time holding a beer. So he was at least twenty-one, which came as something of a relief, both legally and in terms of Buster's self-image. This time The Boy merely grinned and nodded, barely slowing his pace.

So that was that. That. *The Boy will remain a mystery forever,* he thought. It would still be another ten minutes or so before Scissor Sisters took the stage.

And now he's watching The Boy, the cute one who'd complimented his glasses, whom he wishes had been flirting but probably hadn't been. The Boy, his thin arms waving in the air, is pretty close to him now. And beside him is another young man Buster had seen earlier, blond, compactly muscular, stripped to the waist, his face just a bit on the pugnacious side. Not as cute as The Boy, no, but he would do.

In fact, the two young men aren't just side by side, they are, apparently, together. Because they turn to one another, stop dancing for one long moment, and kiss. And not just a friendly peck. Buster can tell, even from a moderate distance, even illuminated just by the lights on the stage, that it's a deep, sexy kiss. The kind he and Charlie used to share, but only in private.

Those teenage girls are back on the stairs again. "I told you twice already," Buster yells over the music. "Off the stairs!" And when he looks back into the pit, the two youngsters have moved on, both literally and figuratively. They're closer to him now, The Boy leaning up against a wall. And they're really going at it, face-to-face, mouth-to-mouth, hands groping everywhere. Buster is a bit envious, a bit erect.

He's also—he has to remind himself—still at work. He checks to make sure everything is okay in his area, which prompts a short trip to clear some folks who are dancing in the aisle. And when he gets back to the head of the stairs, things have gotten, incredibly, even hotter. Now, despite the crush of the crowd, it's pretty obvious that Pugnacious is jacking off The Boy. Which means that The Boy has his dick out. Buster strains for a better angle, but to no avail. He could, of course, grab his flashlight and dive into the pit himself, maneuvering over to catch a glimpse of the skinny boy's cock without arousing particular suspicion. Or maybe not. Maybe it would be too obvious, too awkward if The Boy were to spot him. He's still pondering whether to take the first step when he feels a tap on his shoulder. It's his supervisor. "Want to take a break?" Rachel asks, just audible over the omnipresent throb of sound.

"No thanks. I'm fine here."

Once the supervisor is safely out of sight, Buster walks over a few steps to his right and looks in the two boys' direction. The crowd has shifted, and so have the two young men. Now it's pretty easy to see that both of them have each other's cocks in their hands, jacking each other off as they kiss passionately. As the crowd swirls around them, barely seeming to take note, they cling to each other. Buster once read, he seems to recall, some old porn story about a guy cruising a cute boy in a mosh pit. This is better than that and for real. He thinks it's the most romantic thing he's seen in a long while.

Buster thinks *Yes, I know that most straight people, maybe even some Respectable Gays, would look askance at whipping it out at a concert, much less at thinking of that as "love." But fuck it. Breaking the rules: it's one of the best things about being queer.* He remembers back to when he and his pal Don watched an arty, sensitive movie about doomed poet John Keats and the woman who loved him. In the midst of one heavy-breathing scene of thwarted desire, Don turned and said, "Wow. Back in the olden days, people sure behaved weirdly because they couldn't just fuck."

The mutual masturbation continues. Buster is hornily riveted. He's also a bit envious. Charlie is, after all, gone. His youth is gone, too. And his chances with The Boy? Nil. So...

Oh, fuck, he can actually see their dicks now. And he was

wrong, thoroughly wrong, about the size of The Boy's cock. It is, if not enormous, at least huge. And Pugnacious is pretty equally endowed. Not that Buster is in any sense a size queen. But still...

And that's when something happens that truly astonishes Buster. As a jubilant, stoned, drunk crowd swirls around them, Pugnacious drops to his knees and starts sucking The Boy's dick.

Buster wants to weep. He wants to jack off. He wants to be Pugnacious, sucking The Boy's cock. He wants Charlie back.

The mob in the pit erupts in cheers and applause as Scissor Sisters leave the stage. It's time for the encore, but the fellatio continues. Buster's a bit concerned for the boys' safety; it's not the most ideal place to give head, nor the safest spot to get it. But as the first few people begin leaving the pit, some of them glancing over to the twosome, not one complains to Buster that there's passion transpiring in the pit.

After a minute, Scissor Sisters retake the stage. Jake Shears is half-dressed as a horny Minotaur, Ana Matronic done up as a glamorous toreador, complete with flowing scarlet cape.

Buster realizes it will only be ten or fifteen minutes before the music ends and the lights come up, but the blow job heedlessly continues. Buster can see, in the illumination provided by the flashing lights from the stage, that The Boy's head is thrown back, a blissful expression on his face, his hands on Pugnacious's blond head.

There's a commotion somewhere in Buster's aisle. He tears his attention away from the twosome and goes to straighten things out. When he comes back, Pugnacious is back on his feet and the two have apparently put their dicks away, which is a good thing: as the final strains of "I Don't Feel Like Dancing" fade away, followed by thunderous applause, the houselights come up.

Backing away from the stairs, Buster watches the two for a minute, but then loses sight of them amid the flood of fans emerging from the pit. When he sees The Boy again, Pugnacious is nowhere around. Maybe they were indeed strangers in, as Frank Sinatra would have said, the night. Maybe they've made a date to meet later, perhaps outside the theater. Or maybe the two are in fact boyfriends, and Pugnacious has gone to rescue their jackets from the coatroom. Does it really matter?

Buster manages to catch The Boy's eye, and the kid makes his way over. He's smiling broadly. Buster's glance furtively checks out the kid's crotch. No lingering erection to be seen.

"Hey," says The Boy.

"I've got to tell you," Buster says, "that I've been working here for over fifteen years, and that's the very first time I ever saw a blow job in the pit."

The Boy's grin becomes even wider. Buster imagines kissing those lips. "Was it good?" The Boy asks.

"Magnificent," says Buster.

The Boy throws his arms around Buster and holds him tight. Just for a second. Then he lets go and is on his way, up the aisle and into the night.

Love, Buster thinks, *it's wonderful. Right, Charlie?*

THE BACHELORS

Gregory L. Norris

Episode One

Dudes, everywhere you turned. *Bachelors*, an army of dicks, dicks in crisp suits and wingtips, and one with a T-shirt worn under a tuxedo jacket. That dude, that Bachelor-dick, wore black high-tops with cobalt blue soles. It set him apart from all the other Ken dolls and clones, all the other cocks in this intoxicating sausage-fest, thought Jake. He didn't particularly care for High-Tops, whose name was Brody or Brendan or some other trendy he-man jock's name beginning with *B*. There was something about him that, though flashy, spoke of a lack of genuineness.

Still, Jake shook the man's hand. He shook a lot of hands, hands familiar with jacking on an equal number of dicks, scratching at meaty, low-hanging ball-bags; hands set to play a month-long game to win the right to finger-fuck the hole of the hot blonde called Ami, this season's Debutante. Until fingers were granted permission to go there, Jake figured all those hands would be soaping up dicks in the Dude Ranch's showers or under cover of darkness. Anywhere a dude could find a little private dude-time away from the cameras.

Jake resisted the urge to scratch his balls or adjust his dick, as others were doing, establishing their Alpha-maleness. The army of dudes, of dicks, formed a column twenty-five strong. The mix of colognes and the natural smell of men, of real men, infused the air with hypnotic, potent energy. Jake's dick reacted in the same way that dicks in locker rooms tend to, swelling into a half-hard state. His balls melted and sank halfway to his knees in his black dress pants. Locker-room boners, he knew from playing hoops and summer league baseball, were common practice when a dude drank in the powerful musk of his fellow competitors. One of the Bachelors, Jarod, had gotten a taste of the major leagues for two seasons and had probably popped his share of boners in the clubhouse. He'd likely jerked off in the showers, squirting his nut discreetly in a cascade of soapy bubbles. Another, Chris, claimed to have played football in college. Lacrosse, too. Dude was tall and trim in his designer suit. Jake believed him. The cameras turned in their direction. Jake's dick pulsed. He reached into his pocket and discreetly tucked it down, hoping the lenses were more interested in High-Tops or the baseball god or the rest of the walking dicks with feet. The testosterone in the air was tangible, a smell of real men having real-man conversations, thinking real-man thoughts: sports, beer and, above all, the Debutante, the prize that awaited the last dick standing at the end of the game.

"Hey, dude," a voice growled behind him.

Jake turned to see a youngish man, probably mid-to-late twenties, if he had to guess. Tall, but not gigantic like the former football and lacrosse dude. Dirty-blond hair, bright blue eyes, and a smile that instantly earned Jake's attention, as well as Jake's dick's, which wiggled out of position and back to the front of his pants as he accepted the offer of a handshake.

"Jake Collins," he said, meeting the hand, which the dude would use to milk millions of individual sperm, squirting them down the drain or into the sweaty cotton of a dirty sock over the course of *Dudes and the Debutante*. He matched the other Bachelor's smile.

"Kasey. Kasey Alden. Nice to meet you."

Jake tipped the man his chin and held on to the shake, liking the warmth and strength in the dude's grip. "Hope you feel that way at the end of the show."

"Truly. So what's your story?"

The camera was back in his face. "I run a landscaping business in Colorado," Jake said, mugging it up. One of these dudes would get sent packing, become a fan favorite, and be cast in next season's *Boy Next Door and the Bachelorettes*, the flip side of *Dudes and the Debutante*. Just in case, Jake figured it wouldn't hurt to make the most of his face time.

"You?"

Their hands separated. "I'm an airline pilot," Kasey said.

"Seriously?"

Kasey mugged, too, by indicating the set of pilot's wings pinned to his lapel.

"Good deal, dude," Jake said.

"So, have you met Ami?"

"Not yet, but I'm anxious to. Like every other dude here."

"You want a drink?"

Jake drew in a breath. His lungs filled with Casey's scent, a masculine mix of clean skin, deodorant, and a man's soap, green in color and packaged for rugged Irish rogues. "Sure, that would be great."

Kasey returned with two longnecks and handed one to Jake. "Cheers."

"To the Debutante," Jake said. Their bottles clinked together.

Jake knocked back a swig and caught Kasey's eye on him. The way the other man's throat knotted under the influence of a decent swallow made Jake's balls sag farther, and his dick stiffen fully.

By night's end, the bloodbath was complete. Ami the Debutante pinned Bachelor Buttons on fifteen of the eligible Bachelors' lapels and sent the other ten packing. Both Jake and Kasey survived the massacre, as did the baseball jock, the Giant, the dude in the high-tops, and a house full of proud peacocks, most of whom, Jake imagined, would pump their loads later that night into discarded socks and top sheets as the long, otherwise dry competition commenced.

Episode Two

He and Kasey paired up as roommates and were joined by High-Tops in what came to be known around the Dude Ranch as the Blue Room. And it was blue, all right—Jake's nuts ached for release, but he didn't dare act on his impulses, beyond giving them a tug. First night in a strange bed, in an unfamiliar town, and he rightly assumed that neither Kasey nor High-Tops—Baxter was his name—would have an easier time of passing out than he.

"You asleep?" Kasey asked, his voice barely above a whisper.

Jake rolled over. His cock complained mightily at being driven into the mattress without the benefit of a decent stroke. "No, dude, you?"

"No, can't sleep."

"Same here."

"*Fuck*," Kasey sighed. "She was smoking hot."

Jake reached a hand into his boxer-briefs. Precome coated his fingers. "Truly, dude. Wish we'd gotten more face time."

"Yeah, or one of those one-on-one dates. Maybe tomorrow."

"Maybe tomorrow," Jake said.

"Maybe you two dickheads will stop yammering so I can get some sleep," Baxter grumbled from the third bed in the Blue Room.

They maneuvered around one another in perfectly coordinated steps. Kasey showered while Jake brushed his teeth.

"Hope we're both wearing Bachelor Buttons, bro," Kasey called out from behind the shower curtain.

Jake smiled, tipped his gaze up and focused on his reflection: his baby-blues, a shade grayer than Kasey's, his classically handsome face with square jaw, his neat chestnut hair in its athlete's cut. Bare-chested, he admired his torso with its T-pattern of hair. It was clear why he was still here. Ditto for Kasey.

"You'd better be," Jake answered between foamy spits.

Kasey chuckled into the water stream. Jake tried not to think of him in there, soaping his balls, pulling on his dick. They'd both gone to bed in their underwear, Kasey wearing tighty-whities that showcased magnificent legs and big bare feet that were sexy in a way that particular part of another man's anatomy wasn't supposed to be. Jake's cock strained beneath his towel.

"You almost done in there, dude?"

"Maybe," Kasey said, mischief clear in his voice. "If you're in that much of a hurry, come on in and we'll conserve water."

Jake closed his eyes. Visions played out, rapid-fire, superimposed on his inner eyelids.

"I'd be afraid to drop the soap," he said lightly through suddenly desiccated lips.

"That's right, you'd better be afraid." Kasey drew back the curtain, a smirk on his face. In the mirror, Jake watched the other man perform a helicopter-motion with his dick. That dick, wreathed in lush pubic hair, stood stiffly above a decent-sized sac of nuts, a pair of twins as loose and impressive as Jake's.

"Don't tempt me," Jake joked.

Truth was, Kasey had already tempted him. Jake wore his coolness well, but the emotions swirling secretly inside him were as confusing as they were exhilarating. In a short time, he'd come to like this Bachelor-pilot as much as the best of wingmen past. It was easy to like Kasey, and Kasey—still rotating his dong in clockwise turns above his balls—had made it clear he felt similarly. Not every dude was this easy to get along with, or so effortless to share a bathroom with.

Baxter wasn't.

"When the two of you are done jerking each other's chains, I'd like to get in there and make myself irresistible for the Debutante," the third wheel called through the closed bathroom door, tossing verbal cold water on their brief morning fun.

Kasey stopped helicoptering. Jake willed his dick to soften because, sure enough, there was a camera waiting just outside the door.

On Jake's way out of the bathroom and Baxter's way in, Baxter said, "Why don't you two dudes get a private room?"

Later Jake realized, as the men gathered in the Dude Ranch's lounge, that calculated comment made perfect sense.

There would be a group date, host Errol Powers announced. Six of the fifteen would join Ami at French Chalk, one of L.A.'s finest eateries.

Chris and the baseball dude high-fived. Fists pumped, as did chests. The men gathered in groups of four or more, contenders drawing together. Baxter, an aspiring hip-hop recording artist, and a guy with big spiked hair, the two obvious lone wolves, stood alone.

Jake and Kasey moseyed toward one of the foursomes where Chris, Baseball, and two of the proudest peacocks waited in anticipation of the Debutante's arrival. At this fine, early hour, shorts, scruffy faces, baseball caps, hairy legs and bare feet were the norm. The scent of maleness hung stronger in the air than during the previous night, undiluted by cologne.

"Gentlemen," Kasey said.

Chris tipped his chin, that universal gesture between dudes. "Boys, how's it hanging?"

"Good," Jake said. "Just eager to find my name on that group date card."

"Yeah?" Baseball asked, a cocky smile on his handsome mug. "Because we figured with you and him and your, you know, *bromance*..."

Jake's face screwed into a scowl. "Huh?"

Chris wrapped an arm around Jake, the other around Kasey, and pulled them into a hug. "Hip-Hop over there, that dude..." He indicated Baxter. "He's spreading rumors that the two of you are sweet on one another."

Jake extricated himself from Chris's bear hug and pulled Hip-Hop/High-Tops Baxter aside. The cameras followed. "What the fuck's your problem?"

"It was a joke, nothing serious. It's just that you two nutbags have been joined at the hip since you met. Hey, I'm kind of jealous. Nobody here likes me."

"And you wonder why?"

Ami appeared, dressed in a flowing sundress with a revealing peasant top, and the confrontation shorted out. She handed the date card over to Errol Powers, who read the names: Chris, Baseball, Spikes, the construction worker dude, the Cowboy and High-Tops.

"At least we'll have some peace up there," Kasey said, spinning lemons into lemonade.

They hung out, talked, ate a quiet meal in their shorts and bare feet with the rest of the dejected dudes and, later that night, got Bachelor Buttons in the elimination ceremony, while two more dudes saw their Debutante dreams die.

Episode Three

"I think he's shady," said Kasey.

Jake narrowed his gaze on the bathroom door, through which the sound of running water and off-key singing filtered out. "You think?"

"Dude, none of the other guys like him."

"That's because Baxter is the worst kind of cocksucker—the kind that doesn't suck cock."

Kasey laughed. "True, that. I heard him talking the other night after he got back from the big group date. On the phone. To a chick, I think. Telling her he was only doing this for publicity. To get his career going."

Jake said, "For real?"

Kasey nodded and scratched at his balls, one of which hung openly along the inside leg of his tighty-whities. Big, hairy low-hanger, meaty and red from being scratched. Jake's gaze fell into its pull.

"Dude," he sighed.

"Yeah, I'm gonna tell her, if she gives me some damn alone time today. She needs to be protected from this dickhead."

Jake broke the spell and glanced up, into Kasey's beautiful eyes. "Let me tell you something, good buddy. You *make* the time to be with her, to tell her. If the Debutante is as smart as she seems, she'll listen to you, and you'll get today's one-on-one with her. You deserve it."

"Thanks, buddy," Kasey said, tucking his nuts back into

place. As he did, his meaty dick made a brief appearance.

The shower, the bad singing, ceased. Hip-Hop Baxter exited the bathroom, a bath towel wrapped around his waist.

"Time to dress up pretty—I'm gonna win that one-on-one date," he said, all cocky, the cocksucker.

A platoon of dicks surrounded the hot piece of ass, Ami Addison, the eleventh Debutante. The men drank coffee, juice, water, when it was quite clear by the lumps in their board shorts and blue jeans that what they really wanted to be lapping on was the Debutante's pussy.

"You look amazing," said Baseball, offering Ami a cup of joe.

She accepted, her body language impossible to misread. Ami was in heat and wandering around what amounted to a modern day stud farm. You couldn't swing your dick, thought Jake, without hitting a dozen other dude's dongs.

Chris, the big guy, massaged her bare shoulders. Baseball rubbed her feet. The cameras caught it all in bright and sunny, sexy detail. Ami moaned. Jake figured she would sound pretty much the same when one of the bulls had his tongue or his dick inside her.

Kasey marched over, bold and also confident in his presentation. "Ami, would you do me the honor of spending a few minutes with me?"

Ami extricated herself from the other dudes, who looked none too happy at being third-wheeled and cock-blocked. "Why sure," she said, all smiles. She wrapped an arm around Kasey's and walked away with him, to the Grotto.

"I want to tell you something. I think one of the men here is a snake and that he's playing a dirty game at your expense."

Ami's eyes widened. "Who?"

"The hip-hop artist, Baxter," Kasey said. He explained the rest of what he'd overhead. "I don't mean to sound like a snitch, but I wouldn't be able to live with myself unless I did all that I could to guard your heart from a man who's here with hidden motives."

"That's not being a snitch," she said. "It's being a gentleman, and I appreciate that."

She thanked Kasey, stood, and crossed to the gazebo in a corner of the Dude Ranch's pool area, where the lone wolf waited. The cameras chased her.

"Can I talk with you?" the Debutante asked Baxter.

"Sure, babe, of course," he said, flashing a length of perfect white teeth.

The conversation, Jake guessed, went something like this:

"They're saying such and such about you."

"No, Ami, they're just jealous and they see me as a serious threat in the competition. They know I'm here because I'm serious about finding true love with you."

"Not because you're trying to jump-start your music career?"

"Music? Hell, babe, I'd give that all up for the honor of being your man."

Jake watched Baxter kiss the back of Ami's hand. Soon after that, Hip-Hop notched the day's lone one-on-one date with the Debutante.

The stress steadily drove him mad. Days of being surrounded by dicks and dudes and one lovely Debutante were days of not being able to act on anything, not even in the shower, thanks to the threat of cameras and Baxter and, worse, Kasey. Especially Kasey because, as much as it shocked him to admit it, Jake really liked the dude. Liked him a lot. Dare he think it? He *loved* that handsome goofball.

Jake excused himself from the gang gathered around the pool under the pretence of wanting to lie down. The cameras were, by and large, following Ami and Baxter as they scaled rock walls together or surfed (and turfed), or took in some sporting event in a luxury skybox. Truth was, he needed to bust a nut. And desperately so.

He kicked off his flip-flops, peeled off his shirt and unhooked his shorts, leaving them and his boxer-briefs in a pile on the floor between his and Kasey's beds. Under cover of the top sheet, he tugged on his balls. Jake's dick thickened, feeling twice its usual size as it tented the sheet and pulsed under its own power. He hawked a wad of spit onto his forefinger and thumb and rolled it over his erection. A pearl of juice dribbled out of his pee-slit, adding to the lubrication. He began to pump. An electric sensation jolted his body, teasing Jake's most sensitive flesh. Earlobes and throat, nipples and nuts, asshole and toes reacted favorably. Moaning, Jake extended his legs and flexed his feet. The toes of his right size-twelve slipped free of the sheet and hung over the edge of the mattress.

In Jake's mind's eye, he imagined Ami's pussy, shaved and pink, growing wetter as his tongue swirled around the opening. But the vision was fleeting. As more precome flowed and Jake's cock savored the attention he'd denied it since arriving at the Dude Ranch, the fantasy shifted. Suddenly it wasn't Ami's pussy, but the tight, muscled buttocks of his favorite roommate that he fantasized eating. He'd munched a chick's ass before and figured a dude's wasn't much different, just hairy. Jake loved licking ass. Jake loved Kasey. In his thoughts, he lathed the other dude's ass and tickled his meaty low-hangers with tongue and fingers, and finally moaned Kasey's name.

The timing couldn't have been worse. Or better, depending upon one's outlook.

"Oh, dude, I'm so sorry," Dream-Kasey answered.

Only Dream-Kasey had leapt out of Jake's mind and was now standing at the bedroom's open door.

"*Fuck*," Jake huffed while drawing the sheet tight around his body and snagging his dick at an awkward angle in the process.

Kasey lingered at the door. "Don't stop, man. If I hadn't done the same thing this morning while you and that dickhead were sawing logs…"

Jake drew in a deep breath. Being caught in the act of rubbing one out had a curiously exhilarating affect. But totally, his Inner Jake reminded him, because it was Kasey who'd walked in on him. He felt safe with this dude. Safe, and…

"In fact," Kasey said, walking into the room and locking the door behind him. "Just so I don't feel guilty for interrupting, let me help out."

"Help out?" Jake parroted.

"It ain't what you think. Trust me."

Kasey moved to the side of the bed, dropped down, and seized hold of the bare foot hanging over the edge of the mattress. Electricity pulsed up Jake's leg and tickled his balls.

"What the fuck are you doing?"

Kasey repeated the request for Jake to trust him, and Jake did. What followed was unexpected—and completely amazing: Kasey began to massage Jake's foot, rolling his thumbs in circular motions into his sole.

The back of Jake's skull slammed into the pillow. "Oh, fuck…"

"Yeah, when you fly as much as I do, you learn to appreciate a good foot rub after all those long hours with your feet on the pedals of a bucking beast."

Jake's cock attempted to jump off his body and run away. Only the sheet kept it trapped and attached. "That's un-fucking-believable!"

"Oh, it gets better. Why don't you, you know, keep going while I show you a little bit of heaven."

Jake couldn't believe what was happening, or that it felt so right. "I trust you," he sighed, the words emerging on a happy puff of breath.

He unhooked his dick and cast the sheet aside. A gust of air swept over his shaft and teased the hair on his balls.

"You should. You can always trust me, buddy."

Kasey's hands moved higher, up to Jake's toes, and massaged each one as if stroking a smaller version of cock. Jake's hand worked his dick, and he realized that the pulsations of its sensitive nerve endings were matched by the sensations in his toes.

"You're fucking incredible, dude," Jake moaned.

"So are you," Kasey said.

Jake forced his head off the pillow and focused on Kasey, a vision of baseball cap and blue eyes and flashing smile, and the last of Jake's hesitation melted. "Do you even know how awesome you are?"

"Yeah," Kasey said, "because this other fine dude keeps telling me I am."

That did it. With Kasey's fingers casting magic between his toes, Jake's stroke-hand pushed him past the edge. The room phased out of focus. "Oh, fuck, here it comes!"

Kasey's fingertips traveled up and down his soles, tracing little thunderbolts into his flesh. The other hand caressed Jake's leg, above the ankle, conjuring ecstasy from his hairy shin and calf.

"Do it, buddy. Squirt that cheese all over yourself."

Jake grunted a blue streak of expletives as the first blast flew out of his dick, rising at an angle before raining down, splattering his chest. The next landed on his face, in his open mouth, in his eyes.

"Fuck, dude, yeah," Kasey said, his voice musical, his power over Jake absolute.

Two more blasts followed, leaving him drenched in his own batter.

"That's right, pal," Kasey continued, and Jake was sure that he'd keep on shooting, spurred on by the melody of the dude's voice, the electricity of his touch.

But Kasey's raking fingers relaxed, and the wave completed its crash over him. Jake's head fell exhausted onto the pillow and he thought he might pass out from the aftershock. The best lays of his life hadn't come close to a simple foot rub.

Kasey clapped Jake's leg, sniffed his fingers. "Good job, dude."

"You got that right. That was fucking incredible," Jake sighed. Soaked in equal parts come and sweat, he rose from the bed. "What a fucking mess."

"Looks good on you," Kasey said.

Jake noticed the other man was stiff in his shorts. As drained as he was, Jake wanted more, wanted to help his buddy out, as he'd been helped.

"I'll let you get cleaned up and meet you downstairs," Kasey said.

Jake's desire retreated back into the shadows. Dick leaking, tick-tocking and still swollen between his legs, he licked his lips, imagining that the sour clots of sperm were Kasey's. "Thanks, man, seriously."

"No need to. I'm glad we didn't get picked for that one-on-one date."

"Me, too."

Later that night during the elimination ceremony, the Debutante sent the cowboy packing.

Episode Four

"So, what's this 'bromance' all about?" Errol Powers asked. Of course, the cameras swooped in, right up to Jake's unshaved mug.

Jake took the on-the-spot interview in stride. "That's just Hip-Hop over there trying to stir up crap. He's jealous that some of us guys are getting along so well, because nobody can stand him."

He said it loud enough to be overheard.

"Ami does," Baxter fired back.

"She sure does," the host agreed. "What do you say to that?"

"I say she must be tone deaf."

He guessed it was a mistake, but once the words were past his lips, he was stuck with them.

Ami leaned down to hug him, and Jake loved the scent of her perfume—roses, hypnotic. She was beautiful but, though he wanted to fuck her, he had no other emotion for the Debutante.

"Hey, gorgeous," he said, pulling out a chair for her.

"Such a gentleman," she said.

Jake was aware of every eyeball above every swinging dick in the Dude Ranch's lounge upon him. Strangely, now that he finally had the Debutante all to himself, he found that he didn't welcome the attention. Knowing that all those dudes were grumbling and all of their dicks viewed him as a threat held little reward. He neither wanted nor needed the bragging rights to Ami Addison. Since that afternoon's jack- and foot-fest, all he could think about was Kasey.

"I'm a good guy," Jake shrugged, taking the other seat at the bistro-style table for two, designed so that the Debutante could pull dudes aside for conversation and sound bites. The cameras recorded every blink, giggle and snort.

"I want to think that, but how would I know since you seem to be hanging out in the middle, making no effort to get to know me?"

Jake met the Debutante's gaze. "Ami, you are ridiculously beautiful."

She smiled.

"You're questioning my character when what you should be doing is asking about one or more of the other dudes here. There are some sneaky guys in this house, and they're on this show with ulterior motives," he said.

"You mean Hip-Hop?"

"Yeah, him, specifically. Now I know that a regular Joe like me probably doesn't make for very good television..."

"But maybe you'll make an excellent husband, and that's what I'm here to find: my soul mate."

"Me, too," Jake said.

She took his hand. Jake allowed it. Soul mates. Yup, he'd found his, only not at the table for two.

During the elimination ceremony, there were few surprises. Ami pinned Bachelor Buttons on the lapels of Chris and Baseball immediately, her two golden boys. The ones you just knew would be standing at the end after the rest of the cannon fodder were sent packing.

She offered Bachelor Buttons to Kasey, a handful of others, and, with Jake, the construction worker, and Baxter still standing with their dicks on the chopping block, she pinned one on the hip-hop singer in high-tops.

Jake and Construction Dude. *Oh, let it be me that she jettisons*, he silently prayed. He could return to jerking off on a regular, sane basis, free of Baxter or the cameras catching him in the act.

"Jake, would you accept this Bachelor Button?"

Shit, Jake thought. He took the damn flower and lived to play the game another day.

"You just squeaked past, by the hair on your balls," Baxter taunted.

The cameras were still on them, up in the Blue Room. Jake imagined "balls" would be bleeped. "At least I have a pair."

He settled back on the pillow, aware of the sweat, imagining the musky trace of his come that had painted the case as well as his face.

"For now," the dickhead said.

Jake shook his head, tipped a glance at Kasey, who was thumbing through a sports magazine, his sexy bare feet crossed at their furry ankles, and huffed out a sarcastic laugh. He waited for the lights to go out and the cameras to leave before rolling over and grinding his bone into the mattress.

Episode Five

Jake's worst nightmare came true that morning, when the names of the two deserving dudes that would accompany the Debutante on a private picnic were announced.

"And the two are…" Dramatic pause. "Kasey…and Jake!"

Errol faced Jake. So did the cameras. Jake flashed his best face for the audience.

"All right, buddy," Kasey hooted. Then the two men exchanged a bud-hug, chests slamming together, hands clapping shoulders, a respectable distance maintained between dicks. Jake would have loved crossing swords with Kasey, just not with so many people watching.

The other dudes joined in on the congratulations, though it was clear by the group's body language as a whole that most were pissed their names hadn't been selected.

"What do you think of this?" Kasey asked, holding up a stylish but understated polo shirt.

Jake examined the rest of the ensemble: bare chest, slightly bronzed from the California sunlight, coarse hair running in a line down abs, detouring around ring of belly button—*innie*—before plunging into pelt poking up from waistband. Blue jeans, unzipped. Big bulge of balls and meaty tube proudly displayed in tighty-whities. Flip-flops. Bare feet. Fucking sexy toes. Back up to shades, propped on dark blond brush cut. Heavenly distraction.

"I like it," Jake sighed. "I like it a lot."

"Thanks," Kasey grinned. "You're looking really hot, too, dude."

Jake beamed from the compliment while casting a glance at the mirror. Short-sleeve button-down, black with a beige bar across the pecs, untucked for a jaunty presentation. Jeans, white socks, skater-dude sneakers. "Not as hot as you."

Kasey chuckled. "This is gonna be fun."

"Fun?"

"Sure." Kasey pulled on the shirt. "You, me, Ami. Nobody else I'd want to go on a date with."

"You don't think three's a crowd?"

Kasey shrugged, tucked in, zipped. "It just means I get to spend more time with my favorite dude."

"That means a lot to me."

Kasey clapped a hand on Jake's shoulder. His hand lingered.

Fingers massaged Jake's flesh through his shirt. Jake's eyes rolled back into their sockets as far as possible. The electrical charge zapped through is body. His cock stiffened.

"Dude," he sighed.

In a soft, seductive whisper, Kasey growled, "That feel good, pal? You like that? You want me to do the same thing to your feet later?"

"My feet and my...oh, *fuck*."

"What, buddy?"

Jake gave up the ghost. "My dick, dude. My *fuckin cock*..."

He forced his eyes open, reached for Kasey, and crushed his mouth hard against the other man's. Kasey kissed back. They embraced, this time without fear of bumping dicks. Their cocks, like their lips, collided. Jake reached down, knowing he was at his fullest hardness. To his great relief, he found that so, too, was Kasey.

"I'm not..." Jake managed between kisses. "It's just that... *you*..."

"Same here, Jake," Kasey said, caressing the side of his face. "You're perfect for me, head to toe."

Jake released their dicks, reached around, and grabbed Kasey's ass. "I've never done this before. *Dudes*, I mean. But dude, you..."

Their eyes met, and whatever Jake planned to say went unspoken, which was okay because words weren't necessary. In that sliver of an instant, Jake was happier than he'd ever been, happier than he thought possible. This must be a small taste of paradise, he thought.

And then the hell of their present reality knocked on the door, driving them apart.

"Five minutes, Bachelors," Errol Powers said.

* * *

Champagne and strawberries, luscious salads and soft bread with butter and crab cakes and finger chocolates and raspberry pastries—it was the finest spread Jake had ever seen. And yet, ironically, he barely touched any of it. Seeing Kasey's big feet, freed from their flip-flops, on the other side of the tartan picnic blanket, inspired a different kind of hunger, one that didn't involve food.

The limousine ride to the park had been pure misery thanks to the cameras and the Debutante, tittering about how much she was looking forward to spending time with the two dudes. Jake's cock ached. Curiously, so did his heart. Every now and then, he'd catch a trace of Kasey's scent in the sunlight, the clean male smell of masculine skin mixed with soap from the shower; even worse, he glimpsed a look of longing perceptible only to him, and entropy ensued. He hated this. Hated all of it. Except for Kasey.

"You're awfully quiet," Ami said, breaking the pall. "And you've hardly touched your food."

"Just enjoying this incredible day. And all the beauty," Jake said guiltily, avoiding direct eye contact with either of his companions. He stole another glance at Kasey's toes, long and flat, each capped by dark blond threads. So suckable, those toes.

The date continued, mercilessly long. It was like being repeatedly kicked in the balls, Jake thought. He wondered if he'd survive it. Somehow, the clock resumed ticking, the sun set, and the producers shuffled them back to the limousine, sans Ami, who rode in another car, so all could get ready for the next elimination ceremony.

They couldn't talk in the limo because of the cameras. Back at the Dude Ranch, they fielded an endless succession of questions from the other dicks. How was the date? What kind of food? What do you think your chances are now of getting a Bachelor Button, with the elimination ceremony looming mere hours away? Then there was dinner. Showers and dressing in suits followed. And then they were all standing in the military parade rest position, a smaller army of real men and their real dongs, ten strong, facing one Debutante and nine blue flowers; blue like twenty balls, Jake's in particular suffering the hurt the most.

"Kasey, will you accept this Bachelor Button?"

Jake, who stood in the thinning ranks of the undetermined, saw the other man's smile and his guts twisted into knots.

"I'd be honored."

He and Ami kissed. Kasey moved up beside the hip-hop phony, the tall ex-football player, the baseball god and three others who'd survived the guillotine. Tim, the hunky fisherman from Maine, dodged the next bullet. Jake had wanted desperately to go home, to be done with the drama and manufactured reality. To get out of the game, only the game had changed, and Jake wasn't ready to stop playing quite yet because of Kasey.

Ami picked up the last blue flower. As much as he resented watching her fondle the thing, thinking she was holding their blue dicks, their blue balls, in her clutches, he wanted that last Bachelor Button. There was business to finish. That flower was the key to Kasey.

"I'm not ready to let one of you go, even though I'm still not feeling the connection," she said.

The air grew almost too heavy to breathe. Jake sucked in a desperate breath. The tie around his neck became a garrote.

"Jake, will you accept this—"

"Yes," he blurted out, sucking in a deep, cleansing gulp of air.

Episode Six

It wasn't only about the hip-hop dude, but the morning took an early dip into dark territory, and at its center was Baxter, who'd survived all previous axings to date because, and the other Bachelors knew this, the villain of the house made for exciting TV.

The bathroom light roused Jake. The mumble of voices drove away the last sluggishness of sleep, which hadn't come to him easily to begin with.

"...telling you, babe, you're the only one for me. I'm doing this for *us*."

Jake crooked his ear toward the bathroom door.

"I can't stay on this phone...there's cameras everywhere, and dudes with big ears and bigger mouths..."

Jake slid out of his bed and patted the length of hairy leg jutting out of the covers of the closest bed. "*Kasey.*"

Kasey stirred. "Yeah, dude?"

"Shhh," Jake said. He leaned closer, tried to ignore the intimate scent of Kasey's skin, his breath. "It's that dickhead—he's at it again."

"Baxter?"

"Yeah, and his woman. He just said some shit about being on the show to better their sitch."

Kasey sat up, stirring the heady mix created by bare skin and bedroom feet. "That fucker."

The conversation from behind the bathroom door shorted out, its nearest culprit alerted by the groan of Kasey's mattress. Jake held a finger to his lips, mouthing silence. He was back in the bed by the time the light switched off and Baxter slinked into his. Stagnant pressure settled over the room. Jake waited breathlessly for the telltale sounds of Baxter's mattress sagging and his covers settling. Being so close to Kasey yet not having the ability to act on the passion they both felt was beyond cruel.

The shadows weighed down on him. Eventually, the sun crept into the room, but its light only displaced the physical darkness. The psychological shadows engulfed Jake.

He was in the middle of pouring orange juice, feeling nauseous, dressed in a T-shirt and jogging shorts, his bare feet dragging along the kitchen's floor, when the Debutante's voice drilled into his ears.

"Good morning, Jake."

Jake turned to face her and, of course, the cameras. Ami was a vision of youthful pastels and bubbly exuberance. She hugged him and planted a kiss on his cheek.

"Hey, you."

Ami said, "I thought I'd join the Bachelors for breakfast—and have you all cook for me, of course."

What followed was a nine-man sausage-fest with toes mashing together, chaotic maneuvers to avoid crashing into one another, and general madness, a case of too many cocks in the kitchen. Eggs, bacon, toast, fruit and coffee found their way to the big dining room table. Ami picked at the meal before pulling dudes aside, one at a time, to the bistro table for two. The first to accompany was Baseball. Up next, she walked out the big lummox, Chris, with his Fred Flintstone feet and scruffy face. Last to win an invite to the table was Jake.

"So," she said coyly, urging him to engage in open dialogue.

Jake drew in a deep breath and then just as deeply let it sail. "You're a beautiful girl, Ami, and a smart one. So I just don't get why Hip-Hop Baxter's still here."

"Funny, he keeps saying the same thing about you. Why are you here, Jake?"

He guarded his response. Jake knew the answer, but he didn't want all of America in on the secret. "It sure isn't the same reason he is. I know Kasey warned you about him and what he overheard. Early this morning, I caught some of the same. He was on the phone to what I presume is his girlfriend, saying that he was only doing this for the two of them; that he loved her, not you."

"Do you love me, Jake?"

He didn't, but this was not the venue for such a revelation. "I don't want you to get hurt. Watch out for that dude is all I'm saying."

"Do you have anything else to say?"

Jake shook his head, knowing it signaled the death of his character on the show. It was the end of his six-episode run out of ten on the Eleventh season of Debutantes, dudes, and drama. With that certainty came a measure of relief.

The clock was ticking. He had to act. If he didn't, Jake knew he'd go truly insane.

He found Kasey outside. The cameras were on Ami, who had Hip-Hop's arm tangled around her. Leaning in, he whispered, "Meet me upstairs."

Saying that and nothing more, Jake turned and marched up the stairs to the Blue Room. Once there, he paced. The seconds dragged out with infuriating slowness. Would he have the balls to follow through with it? More balls, his Inner Jake answered, than all the dicks downstairs combined. Oh, yes, he sure would!

Kasey entered the room, and Jake did.

"Dude," Kasey, beautiful Kasey, said.

"I came here looking for love," Jake said. "I'm leaving here certain that I have found it."

Kasey smiled. Jake walked over and followed up words with actions by laying his smile over Kasey's. The two men backed against the bedroom door. From the corner of his eye, he saw Kasey lock it. It was a very good sign.

"I feel the same way, Jake," Kasey said. "I'm so at ease around you. I want to make more effort, only..."

Jake's euphoria deflated. Only? *Only I'm in love with Ami*, an imaginary version of Kasey said in his thoughts.

"Only it really isn't that big of an effort, because I love you, too."

Jake's worry calmed. "You," he grumbled, all smiles—and all cock. His entire body pulsed in concert with the raging stiffness in his shorts. He reached down and boldly fondled Kasey's thickness, and was rewarded with permission in the form of a manly growl.

"Do it, buddy. It's all yours. My heart. My hard-on. All of me."

Jake slapped another kiss on Kasey's mouth at a crooked angle that encompassed one corner. Then he sank to his knees before the other dude and the other dude's dick. He'd received head plenty of times, enough to know the pomp and pageantry. Tug down shorts. Tighty-whities, too, peeling them off hairy ankles and amazing feet. While there, Jake planted his face on Kasey's right foot. He sniffed and licked, tasting warmth, inhaling the hot, buttery sweat from between the other Bachelor's toes. A real man's smell, because Kasey was a real man.

And what a man, at that.

He had seen Kasey's cock erect, notably in helicopter mode, and those balls! Jake licked at them, nipped them between his lips, one at a time. The funk of jockstraps and men's nuts hit his taste buds, and he couldn't have wanted it more. If any of the dudes with their meaty dicks had suggested such a thing was possible on that first night when there were twenty-five bulls running around the Dude Ranch, Jake would have clocked them. But here he was, sucking on Kasey's low-hangers, loving the act because he loved the actor.

He could follow through with the rest, and he did. Spitting out Kasey's left nut, Jake focused higher, sucked the dude's cock between his lips. Head first, swirling his tongue between suckles, recording details like the slightly salty taste, the rubbery consistency, the *rightness* of it. Deeper, a few inches of shaft vanished into his mouth, then a few more, until Jake's nostrils got close enough to Kasey's lush pubic bush to enjoy its tickle. His chin pressed into Kasey's nuts. Kasey's fingers raked through his hair.

"Aw, fuck, buddy," Kasey grunted. "How the hell did I ever get along before you?"

It wasn't the before that concerned Jake, but the *after*. He was going home, he was sure of it. Kasey would move forward to the next episode's challenge, while Jake would be sent packing.

Jake reluctantly released Kasey's cock. "Tonight is it for me, I guarantee it."

A scowl crossed Kasey's joyous expression. "No, don't say that."

"It's true. But when I'm gone, will you…"

"Will I? You fucking better believe I will. You haven't seen the last of me."

"Promise?" The plea sounded desperate, even to Jake's own ears. But he was.

"Here's my promise," Kasey said, his face growing serious. He hauled Jake back to his feet and aggressively laid a kiss on his lips, one that was almost painful in its intensity. Then he backed Jake over to his bed, pushed him down, and with his dick metronome-ing in concert to his movements, stripped Jake bare.

Jake moaned a breathless, "*Fuck*," the anticipation of what was to follow almost too brilliant to believe.

Kasey jumped into bed in reverse beside him, forming that most comfortable and wonderful position in the history of human sex: the sixty-nine; an all-male yin and yang. A couple of Bachelors. Jake and Kasey.

At one point, Jake licked his way lower, to Kasey's ass. There, he feasted.

It was down to the two of them, Hip-Hop Baxter and Jake, scripted precisely the way he guessed it would be.

Kasey stood with Chris and Baseball and the remaining Bachelors, who'd survived the latest thinning of the crowd. Appropriately, Ami was a bundle of sadness. Her eyebrows knitted together as she lifted the final remaining Bachelor Button.

"Ami, it's time to make your decision," Errol Powers said, urging the drama to move forward.

Ami's doe eyes briefly settled on Jake before darting away, the guilt in them damning. "Baxter, will you please accept this Bachelor Button?"

Flashing a cocky smirk, Hip-Hop High-Tops strutted over. "Hells yeah, babe."

Errol clapped a hand on Jake's shoulder. "It looks like the bromance is over. Take a moment to say good-bye to Ami and the dudes before leaving, Jake."

Jake ambled over and gave the Debutante a friendly hug. "Good luck. You're gonna need it."

"I'm sorry that the spark just wasn't there," she said.

He smiled. "I'm not."

Jake gave Ami's back a pat before turning and walking away. Halfway across the room, Kasey shouted, "Wait!"

All eyes—Jake's, the Debutante's, the host's and the remaining dudes' along with the cameras—focused on the source of the provocative prompt.

Kasey walked out of the line of Bachelors, the line of dicks, and tore the Bachelor Button from his lapel. "If you'd throw over an excellent dude like Jake for a lying sack of shit like *that*, I don't want to be here."

Errol Powers faced the camera. "It looks like the bromance is back on."

Kasey marched up to Jake. "Let's get out of here."

Jake smiled and nodded. He didn't care if the cameras caught the look of pure joy showing on his face.

They rode away from the Dude Ranch in the limousine with the cameras pointed at them, two Bachelors and their bags headed for LAX.

"I was never really in love with her," Kasey said. "I mean, she's nice and she's beautiful and all that, but I wasn't gonna stick around if he was. But she'll get schooled on Hip-Hop Baxter, you watch and see."

They pulled up to the curb and got out of the limo. The cameras turned away, now shunning a pair of dudes who had been handed their dicks, at least on the surface.

"So," Kasey said, rocking on his heels.

"So," Jake said in response. "You didn't have to do that."

"Yes, I did. And I wanted to."

Jake's smile widened. "You're fucking wonderful."

"And you're the best, so…"

"So, want to trade that ticket in, get one to Colorado, preferably on my flight?"

"I was waiting for you to ask, dude."

Bachelors no more, they walked away together, beginning a new episode, one with no cameras but plenty of real passion.

CINEMA LOVE

Aaron Chan

"I didn't know there'd be this many people waiting in line on a Friday night."

"Before this, you thought any movie made before 2000 was an old movie," Chris said. "Clearly, you don't know a lot of things."

Not witty enough to throw an insult back at him, I sigh, breath blowing out like a train releasing its last bit of steam. While I counted at least twenty heads in front of us—those were only the ones I could see—there was still a steady stream of people arriving behind us, like a game of snake.

"I'm just saying. Old movies are old. They had their run in the theaters, so they should let new movies have their turn. It's only logical."

Chris snorts, loud enough so that a few heads turn toward us.

"Yeah, it's only logical that the world-changing cinema of *Twilight* take precedence over run-of-the-mill classics," he scoffs. "Besides, I thought you guys were supposed to be into Judy Garland."

"I've heard of her."

"You have much to learn, Young Padawan."

"Huh?"

Chris shakes his head and puts a hand on my shoulder, feigning consolation. "I'm so glad you're here."

Heads and hair ahead of us bob up and down as we finally shuffle forward, the scuffing of sandals and shoes a sweet melody.

"So what exactly is this movie about? All I know is there's a wizard, some singing, and 'Over the Rainbow,' 'cause they sing that all the time on 'American Idol,'" I say as I take out my wallet to pay, combing through wrinkled old receipts to see if I have enough change to not break a twenty.

"Uh-huh. Well, I'm not gonna ruin it for you."

I groan audibly, not caring if anyone hears this time.

"Chris."

"Dude, you'll see in, like, twenty minutes. Jesus." Then he turns his attention to the ticket booth in front. "Two for *The Wizard of Oz*, please."

"Sure thing."

They say the eyes are the window to the soul, but I find it more accurate to say that the voice is a door into the soul. You can look all you want through a window but by opening a door, you have the ability to get inside a person. Every word they choose, every topic they avoid—they are all hints at their character, their past, their education.

Not to mention there are some pretty hot voices in the world, too. And those two words—"sure thing"—were definitely up there: a soft-spoken yet confident, smooth clarinet baritone. His would've made a great jazz-singing voice.

I look up from raiding my wallet. The first thing that stands out to me are the ticket seller's green eyes; it's like looking at two mint leaves. His hair is gelled, the front parted across his forehead to the right side. An indigo shirt highlights his light complexion while a black tie and two thin, black suspender straps contrast with the blue.

He looks as if he stepped straight out of the forties or fifties, or some other past era; old-fashioned but oddly stylish at the same time. He hands Chris a ticket then looks at me. I glance at Chris.

"You're not paying for my ticket?" I ask. Though I hadn't expected him to.

"I asked you to come, but I didn't say I'd pay," he says with a grin. Typical Chris.

I slap the twenty on the counter. Ticket Guy looks at Chris for a sec, then back to me with a "That's what friends are for?" shrug before handing me some coins and the ticket.

"Thanks."

Chris's elbow nudges me in my side. "I'm going to pee. Get some good seats, 'kay?"

Before I have a chance to respond, Chris marches around the corner, leaving me with the crooning clarinet.

"Sorry. He's usually that crude." I gesture to the departed Chris.

"Ah, that would explain it. Oh, well." He smiles, his mouth hooked slightly to the left, lopsided.

"I get the feeling you've never been here before," he continues.

"Is it that obvious? I always pass by but, no, never been in. My friend's in a film class at school and some of the films he's studying are playing here, so part of his assignment is to come and watch them."

"Oh, so you're—"

"He's my best friend. Straight best friend," I add, seeing how he'll react. He only nods.

"So you were wondering about the movie?" His clarinet voice serenades me again.

"Uh, yeah." My, what a charmer I am.

"Well, I don't want to give anything away, but it's a family film with a lot of heart in it. Plus, the Technicolor must've been amazing back when black-and-white was still standard."

"Wow. My expectations totally just went up."

"And not to mention Ms. Garland, who was only a teenager in the film."

I probably look like he's just spoken Greek. There's a rather obvious throat-clearing behind me, seemingly inches from my ear, and when I turn around, a hefty man wearing what looks to be a toupee and a striped shirt (which only adds to his round-ness) towers over—and around—me.

"You guys want to get a room? Some of us have a movie to catch," he says, glaring scornfully between me and Ticket Guy. I instantly turn red.

"Uh, sorry." I turn back around. "Right. So, uh, thanks. Again."

"Enjoy the show." He leaves me with the image of an upturned grin.

As the houselights come on again and eyes adjust, a murmur of what I assume to be post-film discussion spreads across the audience. I follow Chris as he makes his way out from the row.

"Totally poignant, brilliant storytelling and effects, freakin' awesome music—god! And Judy..." Chris the fan-boy goes on.

"Someone's got a crush."

"Now I see why you gays love her." Chris jabs me in the arm.

I playfully punch him back. "Well, except for you. I can't believe you've never seen this movie." We make our way through the carpeted hallway, the lights brighter than in the theater, a tunnel of transition before we step back out into the real world.

"So what did you think, Mr. I Hate Old Films? Reflect carefully before you speak. As someone in a film class, I have the automatic right to dismiss your opinion as uneducated."

I take a few paces while gathering my thoughts.

"I think it was very...well-done for its time. Nineteen-thirties, right? And surprisingly, there was a lot of warmth to it, even after however many years."

"Hmm, that is...an acceptable response. I suppose," Chris says, with the hint of a grin.

The hallway gives way to the lighted incandescence of the lobby. My eyes naturally wander over to the front counter where Ticket Guy is taking money for the next showing from a woman with white, dandelion-puffy hair. He gives her the ticket, nods and smiles politely to her, then glances at the crowd spilling into the lobby. He sees someone he knows because he suddenly grins, and it's only when he waves my way that I realize that someone is me. I flap my hand back and forth stupidly in return.

"I think Kaz wants to see a different kind of show," Chris singsongs in my ear. I push him forward toward the exit, almost knocking over a woman with dreadlocks and her boyfriend, who is wearing a formal suit, desperate to get both of us out of there before I make a complete idiot of myself.

"Shut the hell up, straight boy."

After that night, I'm more aware of the little theater. I look into the glass doors when I pass by on the bus, hoping to see the boy with the clarinet voice, then realize it doesn't make much of a difference if I'm not going in; he's there a few times, sometimes giving people their tickets, other times staring out at the world, watching.

Salty butter and the ping-ponging of kernels dancing welcome me back. It's another Friday night, another movie with Chris.

Ticket Guy looks up from the register as I step in front of him. He's wearing another dress shirt and tie but with an olive vest on top, his hair still parted to the side.

"You're back," he practically sings, with a slight smile stretching across his face.

"I just couldn't stay away," I smile back.

"You know what you're watching today?"

"Nope, nothing about it. Chris is keeping me in the dark."

Ticket Guy's thick eyebrows arch into a fuzzy hill. "Do you wanna know?"

I put down the money and swallow. "Sure."

He takes my change and deposits it in the register. "Well, it's called *The Apartment*. Jack Lemmon and Shirley MacLaine, who you may or may not have heard of?"

I shake my head. "May not."

"Two really good actors, both nominated for Oscars for the film. Anyway, it's about a guy who lets his bosses use his place—hence, *The Apartment*—to sleep with women so he can get ahead in his job. MacLaine works as an elevator operator in the company who's his friend and love interest but she doesn't know he likes her." His voice glides from word to word, *legato*. Despite all the information he's imparting, I don't feel at all like he's lecturing me or being condescending—unlike, sometimes, Chris.

Ticket Guy hands me my ticket.

"That sounds really cool, actually."

He leans in ever so slightly. "The fact that she doesn't know he likes her?"

"All of it." With that, I leave him and head to the hallway, picturing his angled smile behind me.

"Thanks for bringing me, Chris," I say as we make our way out of the slowly illuminating theater and into the hallway.

"You're welcome." He winks at me. I roll my eyes in response. "Just be honest. Would you have come back if he wasn't here?"

I sigh. I briefly contemplate asking, "Who?" but that'd just be delaying the point.

"Honestly?"

"Yes."

"Honestly...no, because I enjoy making you suffer in small ways, like watching a movie alone."

"Screw you."

"You'd like to, I know, but I don't swing that way for you." We grin like morons and laugh, our voices sucked into the black hole of the soundproof hallway before we get back out to the lobby.

"Well, let's go look for your boy, then."

"He's not my boy," I reply, with an unexpected tinge of sadness.

But there's now a young woman at the register, beaming and crinkling her eyes at everyone who walks in, as if high on life itself.

I feel Chris's hand on my back. "Maybe next time, buddy. We'll come by again." I can only nod, not knowing what else to do or say.

As we make our way to the glass doors, someone taps my shoulder from behind. I turn. It's Ticket Guy.

"Hey. How was it?"

"Hey. It was great. Fantastic. Um, you're not working?" I gesture over to the counter, while Chris glances slyly at the two of us.

"No, I finished about half an hour ago."

"Oh, so you're going home then?"

He looks at the ground, then outside, smiling boyishly.

"Actually…I was waiting for you."

I look into his eyes for a few seconds and then I have to look away before I start flushing red. Fortunately, Chris clears his throat loudly enough for everyone in a ten-mile radius to hear.

"Sorry. This is Chris, my best friend. This is, um…" I almost say Ticket Guy.

"Luke. Nice to meet you, Chris." They shake hands. "And nice to meet you…"

It takes me a second to realize I hadn't actually introduced myself to him.

"I'm Kaslo, but people just call me Kaz."

"That's a great name."

"Thanks. It's actually the name of a town in British Columbia."

"Canada," we both say at the same time, me in clarification and he impressively. I'm startled. It's a small town. How does he know? There's an awkward silence.

Chris the Great Straight Friend saves the day again by yawning exaggeratedly, complete with patting his hand to his mouth. This guy should *not* become an actor.

"Well, I gotta get home…super early class tomorrow…you two have fun though…I'll talk to you later…nice to meet you again, bye," spills out of him in one breath. By "bye" he's a good fifteen feet out the door, almost out of sight around the corner, waving.

"Wow. That's one interesting straight best friend you have," Luke notes. He arches an eyebrow.

"You have no idea."

There's a pause. Silence. Before now, the ticket booth has separated us.

"So...what do you want to do now?" I ask.

"Hm. Whatever." He arches his eyebrow again. So cute.

"Ah. Then might I suggest a walk?"

"A mighty fine suggestion indeed."

"Seriously?"

"Yeah, I'm totally serious."

"How is that possible?"

"Well, I've heard of the movie, of course, and I've seen the trailer and I know what it's about from people talking and all."

"You realize you're probably the only person on the entire planet who hasn't seen it, right?"

"Yep. I was tempted, but I'm sure I can live without seeing blue aliens running around," he says with a grin.

Luke licks a trail of melting vanilla ice cream on his waffle cone, two scoops topped with semisweet chocolate chips and a dash of colorful sprinkles. We're in my favorite make-your-own-ice-cream shop downtown, a few blocks from the theater. I swirl the spoon in my ice-cream waffle bowl and scoop up a mouthful of chocolate fudge with caramel bits.

"Okay, so I gotta ask. Top three movies of all time," Luke says.

"Ack, too hard. Hum...I guess I'd have to say *Eternal Sunshine*, *Lord of the Rings*, the third one, and...I dunno, maybe *The Secret in Their Eyes*?"

Luke cocks an eyebrow at me. "Isn't that Spanish?"

"Argentinean, actually."

He nods. "And here I was, thinking you were the kind of guy who watches trite Adam Sandler movies."

"Just 'cause I haven't seen old movies doesn't mean I watch crappy movies."

"True, true."

"Your turn. Favorite three films."

Luke bites into his ice cream, sprinkles crunching in his mouth like mini-fireworks.

"Well, my top movies change. But right now, I'd have to go with *2001: A Space Odyssey, La Dolce Vita,* and I can't forget *Some Like it Hot.*"

"Hmm. I think I've heard of those ones."

"You should watch them sometime. Classics."

My spoon dives into the waffle bowl again, but I stop short from taking another sweet bite. "Luke, have you seen any recent movies?"

His eyes stay on mine, unblinking. "Not any after 2000."

Right away, my eyebrows furrow. "Why not?"

His tongue wipes his lips clean of vanilla. "Why haven't you seen any films from before 2000?"

"Because...I feel like, well, they were made in a different time, a different era, different customs, people, societies, history. To really enjoy and understand those films, you'd have to put yourself in that time, to be someone living in 1939 or 1960 or whenever, and I have difficulty enough just being here in the present."

Luke nods.

"I feel like I won't be able to understand them or I won't be able to relate to them as much. Plus, the movies seem a bit slower than what I'm used to watching."

"That's fair. A lot of people think the same way, and it's true sometimes. But there are underlying themes that transcend time, that are always relevant."

I look at him, at his neatly combed hair, his wet lips

breaking into an assured smile.

"I guess I hadn't thought about it that way."

Outside, the blue of night settles into the world as people walk past the ice-cream parlor. "So why don't you watch any films released after 2000? I mean, hasn't the theater ever screened any newer films?"

"They have, yes, but I don't watch them. I usually find an excuse—cleaning up, helping with snacks. And, okay, I'm totally going to sound like a hypocrite now, but basically for the same reason you don't watch older films."

"Wait, so you're saying you can't relate to current films when you're living in the present, now?"

"It sounds strange, I know, but sometimes I think I would fit in better in a different era, like the fifties or maybe even the sixties. I feel like an anachronism. Besides, so many movies made today are so bad. Anything from Adam Sandler, for example." He bites into his cone, chewing thoughtfully.

"Yeah, but what about all the good films, the ones that'll become new classics?"

He sighs and lowers his cone. "It's true. I know some fantastic films have been made in the last decade, but it's almost as if there's an inner film snob that rejects them, like I have anti-bodies against even the thought of watching a modern film."

I nod in comprehension. I get it. We're film romantics from different dimensions, separate decades.

"It sounds like bs and it's really stupid," he adds.

"It's not stupid."

"But it's bs?"

I'm alarmed that I've said the wrong thing, but then the right side of his mouth rises, hooking into that crooked, cute grin. We devour the last of our chilled treats, watching people pass. We live in today's moment.

* * *

The windows of towering skyscrapers reflect the sun, scattering rainbow prisms of light everywhere. Downtown is a giant stained-glass church. A breeze tickles my bare arm as I march on.

I'm a man on a mission.

I cross the street, and there it is, the red of weathered brick awaiting me. Only a few people wait in line, and it moves quickly. The young woman who took over from Luke the last time I saw a movie with Chris is working. Her glasses are boxy, the color of raisins.

"One, please." My coins rattle and clang on the metal counter in front of her.

"There you are," she says, sliding the ticket toward me.

"Is Luke working today?"

"Yep. He'll be down in a sec."

"All right. Thanks."

"Enjoy the show." I catch her giving me the briefest of mischievous looks.

Sure enough, right after I put the ticket in my jacket pocket, Luke appears out of a black door marked STAFF ONLY a few feet from the counter. He spots me and waves as he strolls over.

"Hey, Kaz. No Chris today?"

"He said he's seen this one already." I take a breath. "I have something for you." With my left arm behind my back, I present him with a pomegranate origami rose, light and dark at the same time, the precisely creased petals in half-bloom. A mossy green pipe cleaner acts as a stem.

He stares at it, then into my eyes. "For me?"

I nod, and hold it closer. He takes it, our fingers skimming.

"A paper rose," says Luke, finally. He closes his eyes and inhales the scentless offering, then smiles. "Best rose I've ever smelled. Thank you, Kaz."

I say nothing, only nod back.

"I've got a surprise for you too. Follow me." He takes my hand, pulls me to the black door. We go up a softly lit stairway and reach another door at the top with a small window. Stepping inside, I'm instantly struck by how compact the room is, dominated by film projectors and other equipment whose function eludes me.

As I gaze around the room, my eyes visual sponges, I vaguely notice Luke dashing back and forth around the projector.

"You work in this room too?"

"Not yet. I started learning from the guy who's usually in here, as kind of a backup person. Apprentice, I guess."

"That's awesome," I say with the astonishment of a seven-year-old who has seen Orion for the first time through a telescope. I watch him inspecting the projector, squinting at every corner of it.

"You have to tell me how this all works sometime."

"Of course. But another day. Here." He gestures to one of the two office chairs facing the large window overlooking the theater and the screen. The rose lies nearby on a table, still crisp.

I sit down, and he does too. We watch as people settle into the seats below us noiselessly. Aside from the whirring of the projector, everything is still.

"You're staying for this one? Is this it?"

"I want my first time to be special," he says. He turns his head to the right, looking at me. "To be with someone special."

My hand reaches over to his on the armrest, my fingers intertwining with his. I wonder if he feels my pulse through my skin, its accelerated pace. Hummingbird wings.

He squeezes my hand as the houselights dim.

On screen, a fly zips around on a road. *Le trois septembre 1973, à dix-huit heures vingt huit heures vingt huit...*

* * *

We watch as Amélie and the garden gnome spontaneously chase after a man she "has an affinity with" in the train station; as she guides the blind man through the streets in Paris and paints the picture of everything happening; as her face falls when she learns Gina has a meeting with Nino; and finally, the romantic kisses on the eyes between the two leads.

Yann Tiersen's score kicks in again as the pages of the photo album containing pictures and names of the cast flip through. Our hands are still entwined, warm from our collective body heat.

"How was it?" I whisper.

"I, I don't really know what to say after that," he says, watching the credits. Then he turns and looks at me. I gently squeeze his hand and lean toward him, brushing my lips across stubble as I lay a soft kiss on his cheek. I pull back and see that his eyes are still closed, his mouth slightly open. A moment passes.

Slowly, the right corner of his mouth curls upward. There it is again. That smile.

"Whimsical," he replies, and leans in to press his smile into mine.

I would remember that word from then on.

Years later, we would remember how it was a French romantic comedy from 2001 that brought two boys who loved films on either side of the century together.

ABOUT THE AUTHORS

FYN ALEXANDER grew up in Liverpool, England, with a great love of books and the English language. As an adult Fyn moved to Canada, but returns to England to visit every few years to reconnect with his roots. Fyn is also the author of the *Angel and the Assassin* series.

STEVE BERMAN is a romantic, which is why he always wanted to write a story that combined the wonder of a musical with gay love. He hopes it makes you sigh and smile. His young adult novel, *Vintage*, was a finalist for the Andre Norton Award.

AARON CHAN (theaaronchan.com), born and raised in Vancouver, realized he was a true artist at heart when he began taking piano lessons at the age of five. A graduate of Vancouver Film School, Aaron is a writer, musician, filmmaker and a student at Langara College. He also likes cats.

MARTIN DELACROIX's (martindelacroix.wordpress.com/) stories appear in over twenty erotic anthologies. He has published four novels: *Adrian's Scar, Maui, Love Quest,* and *De Narvaez.* He lives with his partner, Greg, on Florida's Gulf Coast.

JAMIE FREEMAN (jamiefreeman.net) lives in a small Florida town. He has published the romantic novella *The Marriage of True Minds* and his stories can be found in *Best Gay Romance 2010, Necking, Sindustry* and elsewhere. He writes in a variety of genres including erotica, romance, science fiction and horror.

STEVE ISAAK, who also writes as Nikki Isaak, lives near San Francisco. He has published two anthologies, *Can't sleep: poems, 1987-2007* and *Charge of the scarlet b-sides: microsex stories & poems.* He contributes to and edits readingbypublight.blogspot.com and microstoryaweek.blogspot.com.

HÅKAN LINDQUIST was born in the small Swedish coastal town of Oskarshamn, where some of his stories take place, and now lives in Stockholm and Berlin. He has written five novels, one opera libretto and several short stories. His novel *My Brother and His Brother* was published in English in 2011.

ANTHONY MCDONALD's four novels are *Orange Bitter, Orange Sweet,* the best-selling *Adam, Blue Sky Adam* and *Getting Orlando.* His stories have appeared in numerous anthologies, including *Best Gay Romance 2011.* He lives in England where he has previously worked in the theater, in just about every capacity except director and electrician.

GREGORY L. NORRIS is a full-time professional writer with work published in numerous magazines and anthologies. He worked as screenwriter on two episodes of Paramount's "Star Trek: Voyager" and is a former writer for *Sci Fi*, official magazine of the Sci Fi Channel. He lives at the outer limits of New Hampshire.

RON RADLE writes gay love stories from the heart of the South Carolina Bible belt. His work has been published under a number of names in a number of places, both literary and nonliterary. He is finishing an erotic romance novel set during his college days in the mid-1980s.

ROB ROSEN (www.therobrosen.com), author of the novels *Sparkle: The Queerest Book You'll Ever Love*, *Divas Las Vegas*, *Hot Lava* and *Southern Fried* has contributed to more than 150 anthologies, most notably *Best Gay Romance 2007, 2008, 2009* and *2010*.

SIMON SHEPPARD is the Lammy Award–winning author of *Sodomy!*, and six other books including the upcoming *The Dirty Boy's Club*, and his work has appeared in several hundred anthologies, including many editions of *Best Gay Romance* and *Best Gay Erotica*. He works part-time at San Francisco's Warfield Theater, and hangs out at simonsheppard.com.

C. C. WILLIAMS (ccwilliamsonline.net), after moving several times about the country and through Europe, is now settled in the Southwestern United States with his partner, JT. When not critiquing cooking or dance show contestants, he is at work on several writing projects.

ABOUT THE EDITOR

RICHARD LABONTÉ (tattyhill@gmail.com), when he's not skimming dozens of anthology submissions a month, or reviewing one hundred or so books a year for Q Syndicate, or turning turgid bureaucratic prose into comprehensible English for the Inter-American Development Bank or the Reeves of Renfrew County, Ontario, or coordinating the judging of the Lambda Literary Awards, or crafting the best croutons ever at his weekend work in a Bowen Island recovery center kitchen, likes to startle deer as he walks terrier/schnauzer Zak, accompanied by husband, Asa, through the island's temperate rainforest. In season, he fills pails with salmonberries, blackberries and huckleberries. Yum. Since 1997, he has edited almost forty erotic anthologies, though "pornographer" was not an original career goal.